"You know what that woman stole from me with her silver bullet. She stole the power of the wolf, the freedom of the night. The thing that happens to me now is my curse for as long as I live."

"Let me stay with you," Roy said. Even before she had claimed him he had been hers. Now they shared the power and the curse, and he was hers forever.

"No. The change . . . I would rather die than have you see the thing I become."

"I love you, Marcia. I would share anything with you."

"Then you can share with me the vengeance against the woman who has destroyed half of me . . . *your wife!*"

It had begun again . . .

THE HOWLING II

Fawcett Gold Medal Books
by Gary Brandner:

THE HOWLING   13824-0 $1.75

THE HOWLING II   14091-1 $1.95

THE HOWLING II

Gary Brandner

FAWCETT GOLD MEDAL • NEW YORK

THE HOWLING II

Published by Fawcett Gold Medal Books, a unit of CBS Publications, the Consumer Publishing Division of CBS Inc.

ISBN: 0-449-14091-1

Printed in the United States of America

10   9   8   7   6   5   4   3   2   1

THE HOWLING II

LOS ANGELES (UPI)—A fire of undetermined origin swept through a narrow valley in the Tehachapi Mountains north of Los Angeles yesterday, virtually wiping out the tiny village of Drago. Firefighters from Los Angeles and Ventura Counties brought the blaze under control early this morning, and had it extinguished before it could threaten any of the neighboring communities.

As yet there has been no reported contact with any of the residents of Drago. Authorities refused to make an estimate on the number of casualties as crews were still sifting through the ashes for victims.

The only known survivors at this hour are Mrs. Karyn Beatty and a friend, Christopher Halloran, both of Los Angeles. Mrs. Beatty's husband was missing and believed to have perished in the fire. Halloran and Mrs. Beatty declined to speak with reporters.

According to U.S. Forest Ranger Phil Henry, the final death toll may never be known. Since Drago was not an incorporated town, no accurate records were kept of its population. It is estimated that between one hundred and two hundred people lived there. So intense was the blaze, which destroyed two hundred acres of timber in addition to the village, that searchers are finding it difficult to distinguish human remains from those of animals.

1

KARYN KNELT ON THE moist grass and worked with her fingers in the dirt around the roots of the rose bush. There were no flowers on the bush, and there should have been. Karyn felt she was somehow responsible. Although David had never mentioned it, she was sure his first wife had been a gifted gardener. That was the trouble with marrying a widower—the departed wife was always good at everything.

As for Karyn, except for her houseplants, which enjoyed a special place in her affections, she had little interest in or aptitude for gardening. Outdoor plants, she felt, ought to be able to take care of themselves. However, David and Dr. Goetz thought getting outside and working with her hands was

good for her, and she did not want to disappoint
them.

While she poked idly at the damp earth, Karyn
let her mind wander. There was vacation time to
be worked out for Mrs. Jensen, the housekeeper,
and a Parents' Day coming up at Joey's summer
school. She smiled, pleased at the commonplace
concerns that occupied her mind these days. It was
a healthy sign, she thought.

Karyn did not hear the soft approach of the
padded feet behind her. The first indication she
was not alone was the huff of warm breath on the
back of her neck. She started to rise, lost her balance, and fell awkwardly to the ground.

She looked up and saw the other face staring
down into hers. Its black lips were stretched in a
canine grimace, the yellowed teeth bared. She
tried to squirm away, but two heavy paws pinned
her as the animal dropped its weight on her chest.

In that instant, all the horror of Drago flooded
back from the closed-off portion of her mind. The
wolfish face with its long, cruel teeth came at her.
She screamed. The weight on her chest lessened
for a moment, and she rolled away, curling herself protectively into a ball. She felt the animal
prod at her, trying to turn her over. She screamed
again.

The back door of the house banged open and
a solid woman with graying, blond hair rushed

out. She ran heavily toward Karyn, still lying on the ground by the rose bushes.

"Bristol, stop that!" the woman called. "Come here, you bad boy."

Cautiously Karyn opened her eyes. A few feet away, Mrs. Jensen stood with her hands planted on her hips. Sidling toward her, a don't-hit-me look in its eyes, was a coltish young German shepherd.

"Shame on you," Mrs. Jensen scolded the dog. "Frightening people like that." She seized him by the collar and tapped him lightly on the nose. "I'm sorry, Mrs. Richter. He's just an overgrown puppy. He wanted to play, that's all."

The back door burst open again and David Richter hurried out. He was a man of forty-eight, with a strong, serious face. He wore a sweater and slacks, this being Sunday, but he never seemed really comfortable without the three-piece suit he wore daily to the brokerage.

Karyn rose unsteadily to her feet. David ran across the lawn to her side and took her arm.

"Are you all right?" he asked.

"I'm fine," Karyn said, still out of breath. "It's nothing."

David turned on Mrs. Jensen, who was still holding the dog by his collar. The dog kept lunging up, trying to lick her face.

"What's that dog doing here?" David demanded.

"It's my sister's puppy," Mrs. Jensen said. "He didn't mean any harm."

"You know we don't allow animals here," David said.

"I was just watchin' the dog for an hour while my sister went to the dentist. She didn't want to leave him alone."

"Well, get him out of here," David ordered. "And don't ever bring a dog to this house again."

"David, it's not that serious," Karyn said. "The dog just caught me by surprise."

"He didn't mean any harm," Mrs. Jensen said again.

"Yes, yes, all right," David said, softening his tone a bit, "but I want him out of here right now."

"Yes, Mr. Richter," she said. And to the dog: "Come along, you bad boy."

As Mrs. Jensen led the dog around the side of the house, a dark-eyed boy of six dashed through the door and across the lawn to where Karyn and David stood.

"What happened?" the boy said, looking from one of the adults to the other.

Karyn ruffled his hair. "It's all right, Joey. I was just startled by a dog."

"A dog?" The boy looked around eagerly. "Where is he?"

"Never mind," said David. "Mrs. Jensen took him away. You go inside now and wash up for dinner."

Joey looked wistfully off in the direction the housekeeper had taken the dog. "Can't I just go and see him? Just for a minute?"

"Inside, Joey," said David. The boy trudged back across the grass and into the house.

"I feel so guilty because he can't have a pet," Karyn said.

"It won't hurt him to do without one. Now let me help you inside. You're still shaking."

"Really, David, I'm quite all right," Karyn said, but she allowed herself to be led into the house.

"Sit down there in the big chair," David said when they reached the living room. "Put your feet up."

Karyn did as she was told.

"Now wait right there and I'll get something to calm your nerves." He went off to the kitchen, and returned a minute later carrying a tall glass.

"Here's a nice glass of milk," he said.

A nice shot of Scotch would do her nerves a whole lot more good, Karyn thought, but she smiled her thanks and took the glass from David's hand.

He stood with his arms folded, studying her gravely as she sipped at the milk. "You gave me quite a scare."

"I'm sorry."

"What a shame that this should happen just when you seemed to be getting better."

Karyn set the glass down carefully on the end table next to the chair. "I hate that expression," she said. "Getting better. It's a consant reminder that I'm a convalescent mental case."

"I didn't mean it that way. It's just that I'm a little disappointed that, after a year, Dr. Goetz hasn't done more for you. Do you think we should try someone else?"

"Dr. Goetz is as good as any of them," Karyn said. "Really, David, you're making too much out of this. The dog came up behind me and took me by surprise. I overreacted, that's all."

"The dog," David said, watching her. "It reminded you of that Drago business, didn't it?"

Sure. *That Drago business.* The unpleasantness in the mountains. Nothing remarkable, really, just fighting off a pack of werewolves and seeing your husband change into . . . Karyn broke off the thought and shuddered.

David moved quickly to her side. "I'm sorry, dear, I shouldn't have brought that up."

Karyn squeezed his hand. "No, darling, it should never become a taboo subject, or I *will* be in trouble. And you're right about the dog. Seeing its face suddenly so close to mine took me back for a moment to Drago. It's been only three years, you know, and we've got to expect incidents like that from time to time."

"And you're still having the dreams, aren't you?"

"Yes," Karyn admitted. "But not so often, any more."

David frowned. "When is your next appointment with Goetz?"

"Tomorrow."

"And you really think he's helping you?"

"As much as anyone could."

David patted her hand awkwardly. "All right, then, we'll go on with him. I just hope he can make you see that this Drago business is all—behind you."

As she lay that night in bed beside her sleeping husband, Karyn recalled his words. She knew that what he had started to say was "all in your mind." She would be happier than anyone to be convinced of that, but it was not so. Drago was as real as the moon outside their bedroom window, and much closer. The werewolves were real too. And somewhere, Karyn knew, one or more of them survived.

Nine hundred miles away, in the grape country of California, another woman lay awake beside her man. Her long, supple body gleamed like old ivory in the moonlight. Across the pillow, her hair spread in gentle waves of glossy black, shot through with a startling streak of silver.

The man stirred in his sleep. The woman quieted him with a hand on his broad, bare shoulder.

"Rest easy, my lover," she whispered. "Soon we will have much work to do."

2

FROM THE WINDOW of Dr. Arnold Goetz's office in the new Farrell Building, Karyn could see the sailboats skimming across Lake Washington under a stiff westerly breeze. It was one of those brightly washed summer days when the dreary months of rain are forgotten and the people of Seattle go outdoors to celebrate the sun.

Karyn stood at the window talking in a flat, emotionless voice. Finally she said, "So that's all there was to it. Just a silly incident with a dog, and it was all over in a minute."

Dr. Goetz waited a full fifteen seconds. It was a technique of his that Karyn recognized. The purpose was to encourage the patient to elaborate on, or perhaps contradict, the last thought. When Karyn did not offer to continue, the doctor spoke.

"There is no doubt in your mind, then, that it was only a dog yesterday."

Karyn spun around to face him. "Of course it was only a dog." She walked over and sat down in the chair facing the doctor's desk. "I was frightened for a moment because it brought back bad memories. That's all."

Dr. Goetz nodded sagely. "Yes, I see. And tell me about the dreams. You say you still have them?"

Karyn bit her lip and frowned. "Yes. And they worry me more than the business with the dog. Will I ever stop hearing it at night, Doctor? The howling?"

"You *do* understand that it is only in dreams that you hear this—howling?"

Karyn leaned back in the chair. Sunlight from the window caught her pale blond hair and made it a glowing frame for her face. She was twenty-eight now, and there were little lines at the corners of her eyes, but the touch of maturity only emphasized her beauty.

"Yes, Doctor," she said wearily, "I know it only happens in dreams. Now. But three years ago in Drago, the howling was real. As real as death."

Dr. Goetz touched his glasses. Karyn had determined that it was his unconscious gesture of disbelief. He put on an understanding smile.

"Yes, I see," he said.

"Bullshit."

The doctor brightened. Gut reactions always encouraged him.

"You don't see at all," Karyn told him. "You don't believe Drago actually happened any more than my husband does. Any more than all the other people I've told about it."

After his customary wait the doctor said, "Karyn, whether I believe or not isn't important. What happened in the past or didn't happen really doesn't concern us. Our bag is the here and now. All that matters to us is how you feel about it."

Karyn met the doctor's sincere gaze. He was having a difficult time making the transition from the traditional Freudian to the trendy transactional school of analysis. Everybody's got problems, she thought.

"What it makes me feel is scared shitless," she said.

Pause.

"Why?"

"Because I know they aren't all dead."

"When you say 'they,' you mean—"

"I mean the wolves," Karyn supplied. "The werewolves."

She watched closely for a reaction—the narrowing of the eyes, or the little quirk, which she had seen so often, at the corner of his mouth. Dr. Goetz held his expression of friendly concern. He was good.

"Do you want to tell me about it?" he said.

"Doctor, I *have* told you about it."

"Tell me again, if you think it would help."

Hell, why not, Karyn thought. There was no pain in the telling any more, and that, at least, was an improvement. Maybe if she heard the story often enough herself it would become meaningless, the way a familiar word repeated over and over eventually becomes a nonsense sound.

She stood up again and walked back to the window. There, watching the peaceful scene down on the lake, she repeated the story of the damned village of Drago, and the six months she spent there with Roy Beatty.

She described the way it began, with the howling in the night. Then there had been the cruel killing of her little dog. She told of the strange people who had lived in the village, and the huge, unnatural wolves that had roamed the woods at night. In a quiet, controlled voice she spoke of the black-haired Marcia Lura, who had bewitched Karyn's husband and finally taken him forever with the virulent bite of the werewolf. Finally she told of the escape from Drago as she and Chris Halloran had fled the burning village.

Dr. Goetz waited, then spoke. "You said they aren't all dead. The wolves."

"As we drove out of the valley with everything behind us in flames, I heard it again from off in the forest. The howling."

Abruptly Karyn stopped talking and went back to her chair across from the doctor. "Telling the story doesn't make it any better or any worse," she said. "All it does is keep the memory fresh. What I want to do is put Drago out of my mind. Now and forever."

"I can understand that," Dr. Goetz said reasonably. "And that's what we're working toward, isn't it? But, Karyn, before we can finally put this idea out of your mind, we have to find out what put it *in*."

Karyn stared at him. She spaced out her words carefully. "What put this *idea* into my mind, Goddamnit, is that it happened."

"Yes, of course," the doctor went on. "Maybe when you were a little girl there was some experience, something ugly, with wolves or large dogs."

Karyn shook her head wearily. "No, Doctor, not when I was a little girl. My only traumatic experience with wolves came when I was a full-grown woman. Three years ago. In Drago. You're telling me the same old thing, aren't you, that it's a delusion?"

"Delusion is a term we don't use much any more. We understand now that things that happen in the mind are every bit as vivid, and often more damaging than what we call reality. I'm sure your experience in Drago is as real to you today as this room we are sitting in. The important thing, as I said—"

Karyn only half-listened as Dr. Goetz droned on in his silky, reassuring voice. He was saying the same thing everyone else did. Namely, that she had imagined the whole Drago episode. Maybe in time he could convince her of that. If he could, he would be well worth whatever David was paying him. In the meantime, it did help a little to be able to talk.

There was a subtle change in the doctor's tone, and Karyn saw his eyes flick over at the discreet little clock on his desk. Her hour was up.

3

KARYN DROVE SLOWLY north over the Aurora Bridge toward Mountlake Terrace, where she and David had their home. Her thoughts, as usual when she left Dr. Goetz, were on Drago and what happened afterward.

There had been one moment of triumph at the very end when she had fired the deadly silver bullet into the head of the black she-wolf. But that small victory, like the escape with Chris Halloran, had lacked a ring of finality. Even as she and Chris had paused to look back on the valley in flames, neither of them had really believed it was over.

For six tempestuous months they had tried to pretend it was, and that they were just another ordinary couple. After sharing the horror of Drago, it had seemed a natural thing to stay together. How wrong they were.

For a time they had traveled aimlessly from place to place, living on pills and nervous energy. Before long their pent-up emotions were turned against each other. At the end of six months these two people, who had shared more in a day than many couples do in a lifetime, were living on the edge of violence. The most insignificant squabble could erupt in an ugly word battle. They were staying in a Las Vegas hotel when the final blowup came.

Karyn had spent the morning in their room. She had the air conditioner turned up full and wore a sweater buttoned to the throat as protection against the dry cold. Chris had gone down to the swimming pool early, after making only a half-hearted attempt at persuading her to come with him.

At noon Chris returned. He glanced briefly at Karyn and went into the bathroom. Not until he had showered, shaved, and dressed did he speak to her.

"Do you want to go down and get some lunch?"

"Can't we have something sent up?"

"Why?"

"I'd rather not leave the room, that's all."

"For God's sake, Karyn, you can't just sit up here and hide from the world like a frightened child."

His words cut into her like a dull knife. She

flared back. "I can do anything I want. Who are you to tell me what I can't do? Nobody asked you to run my life."

Chris's eyes had turned dark and dangerous for a moment, then he whirled and stormed out the door. Karyn fought down the angry impulse to throw something after him.

The rush of blood through the veins made a roaring in her ears. She walked over to the window, parted the draperies, and blinked at the bright white Las Vegas sunlight. Twelve stories down, she could see people in the pool and on the deck around it. Everyone seemed to be laughing and having a fine time. Was she the only one in the world, Karyn wondered, who was miserable?

She let the draperies fall back across the window, and returned to the chair where she had sat all morning. She was still there, shivering with the cold, an hour later when Chris returned.

He closed the door firmly behind him and stood looking at her. "Why the hell don't you turn the air conditioning down?"

"I like it this way."

She could see him start to get angry, then, with an effort, relax.

"Karyn, we have to talk."

"Why?"

"Because we're destroying each other."

"Is that a fact?"

"Cut it out, damn it. I've had all of this I can take."

"Poor you."

"This continual picking at each other is tearing me apart. It isn't doing you any good, either. Have you looked at yourself closely in the mirror lately?"

"Well, thank you very much."

"Will you please stop playing childish games? I know what you went through at Drago, but—"

Karyn sprang out of the chair and faced him angrily. "You have no idea what I went through. You were there only at the very end. I spent six months in that place. Six months in hell."

Chris spoke in a carefully controlled voice. "I know that, Karyn. I know you suffered a lot. What I want to do now is help you."

"Oh? And just how do you think you can help me?"

"It would be a start if we brought the whole thing out in the open and talked about it."

"I don't want to talk about it," Karyn snapped. "Not to you, not to anybody."

"I'm the only one you *can* talk to about Drago," he said. "I am the only person in the world who would believe it, because I was there. I saw the wolves, and I know what they were."

Karyn clapped her hands over her ears. "I don't want to hear. I don't want to think about it. Why don't you let me forget Drago, so it will go away?"

"It will never go away," Chris said. "It will al-

ways be locked in the back of your head. If we
could just talk about it—"

"There you go with your 'talk about it' again.
You sound like one of those fucking parlor psy-
chologists. Tell me, where did you get your medical
degree, *Doctor*?"

"Cut it out. I can't take any more of this."

"Don't then. Don't take a Goddamn thing you
don't want to. Nobody's holding you."

"That's right," he said in a voice that had gone
suddenly cold. "Nobody is."

In thirty minutes Chris Halloran had packed his
clothes and left the hotel. That had been two and
a half years ago. Karyn had not seen him since.

The weeks that followed the Las Vegas breakup
with Chris were fragmented in Karyn's memory.
She knew that during that time she was very close
to losing her hold on sanity. Somehow, she had
made her way back to her parents' home in the
Los Angeles suburb of Brentwood. For two months
she had a full-time nurse, and never left the upstairs bedroom that had been hers when she was a
little girl. The days were blanks and the nights were
filled with shadows where lurked unspeakable horrors.

Then gradually the world came back into focus.
Karyn at last learned to talk about the summer in
Drago. Then as now, no one really believed her,

but they listened sympathetically. She learned that Chris had been right. Talking about it *did* help.

After six months in the quiet, comfortable house with her family, Karyn began to feel whole again. She tried to contact Chris Halloran, but learned he had taken a traveling assignment with his engineering firm, and was seldom in town for long. Maybe, she decided, it was better this way. She would have liked to say she was sorry about the bad days at the end, and keep at least a part of Chris's friendship, but seeing him might just open old wounds.

Instead, she had accepted the invitation of a college classmate and flown to Seattle for a visit. That was when she met David Richter.

David was twenty years older than Karyn, and solid as Mount Rainier. He did not have the dreamy romanticism of Roy Beatty, nor the charm and dash of Chris Halloran, but he was exactly what Karyn needed. She had been a little hesitant about meeting David's son, but she need not have worried. She and Joey hit it off immediately.

The big test, in Karyn's mind, came when she told David the story of Drago. He had listened patiently and seriously, without laughing or patronizing her. He did not, of course, treat it as reality, but accepted it as a minor eccentricity as he might have accepted a slight limp.

David asked her to marry him two months after they met. He offered her security and stability, and a kind of quiet love she had never known. She said yes.

All in all, Karyn was content with her life as Mrs. David Richter. Now if she could just stop dreaming of the wolves, and shake the feeling that someday, somewhere, they were going to kill her.

4

IN THE SAN JOAQUIN Valley of California a band of gypsies made their camp in a clearing at the edge of a forest. Their camp was not much like the romantic fiction of operettas and the movies. Instead of colorful horse-drawn wagons, their vehicles were vans, pickup trucks, travel trailers and campers. The music in the camp came from transistor radios and tape decks, not from the fabled wild violins and tambourines.

Some things, however, remained little changed over the centuries. Although many of them worked for daily wages in the neighboring fields, the gypsies remained wanderers. An entire camp might pack up and vanish one night, to appear next morning in another place miles away. And the gypsies still had their own methods of communication, which carried news between distant camps more swiftly than the mails.

In yet another way these modern gypsies resembled their forebears. They had a deep respect for the old beliefs. They still held that a man's future could be seen in the lines of his hand. The turn of a card could chill the blood like the whisper of Death. And the gypsies knew there were those who existed outside the laws of nature, creatures to be feared and never, never betrayed.

For this reason the gypsies stayed well away from a battered old trailer that rested on blocks at the periphery of the camp. By their heritage they were bound to protect those who dwelt there, but the wisdom of their ancestors kept them wary.

Inside the trailer was shadowed, the sun filtered by green cloth curtains across the two small windows. There was a tiny alcove for cooking, with a butane stove and refrigerator. There were a table and benches, which folded up out of the way when they were not being used. At the far end of the trailer, across its entire width, was a bed, covered with a profusion of pillows, silken scarves, soft blankets over a billowy mattress.

Amidst the pillows and scarves on the bed were the wet, naked bodies of a man and a woman. The man was blond, and broad through the chest and shoulders. The woman was dark and long-bodied, with compelling green eyes and hair of midnight black shot through with a streak of silver.

The body of the man strained over the woman. Her long, strong legs locked him between her knees. With a last powerful thrust the man buried himself deep inside the woman. With a sharp intake of breath, she clasped him tight against her. He groaned deep in his chest. Her teeth sank in and marked his shoulder. They cried out together, and it was finished.

Roy Beatty rolled over on his side. The woman rolled with him, still holding him tightly in the circle of her arms. Roy's breath came in ragged gasps. As always with Marcia, their climax had been a devastating experience, leaving him spent and drained as no other woman ever had. Since the first time he saw her in the hamlet of Drago— had it been only three years?—Roy Beatty had belonged to this woman. He had been hers even before she had claimed him in the ancient way. Now they shared the power and the curse, and he was hers forever.

"Are you at ease now, my Roy?" Marcia Lura let her fingers wander through the damp golden hair across his chest. "Did I please you?"

Roy pulled a breath deep into his lungs and exhaled slowly. "You please me like nothing else on earth."

"And you will never leave me?"

He pulled back his head to look at her. "Leave you, Marcia? Impossible."

"That is good." Her fingers massaged the corded muscles where his neck joined his shoulders. "We will leave this place soon."

Roy pulled away from her and sat up. He ran his hand over the smooth length of her body. "Are you sure you're well enough to travel?"

"I am as well now as I will ever be. I know these have been difficult months for you, my Roy, nursing a sick woman, but now it is over."

"All that matters is having you near me," he said.

"I will always be near you," she said. "I will be all the woman you will ever want. But now, you know what we have to do."

Roy's eyes shifted away. He reached down for his clothes where they had fallen beside the bed. "You mean—Karyn."

"Yes!" Green fire flashed in her eyes. "That woman."

He turned back to face her, feeling the impact of her hatred. "Do we have to go through with this?" he said. "So much time has passed."

Marcia ran her eyes over him slowly. When she spoke there was a chill in her voice. "You can't be saying you still have tender feelings for her. Can you?"

"She was my wife," Roy said.

"Your wife!" Marcia spat out the words. "What did that woman know about being a wife? If she had pleased you, you would not have come to me."

"But it all seems so long ago."

"Does it? Does it, Roy? To me, it seems like yesterday." Marcia touched the slash of silver that ran through her dark hair above the left eyebrow. "I think of that woman every time I look into a mirror and see how she marked me when she fired the silver bullet into my head."

"She was defending herself."

"And now *you* are defending her."

"Marcia, no, I am with you always. You know that."

"And yet you take the part of the woman who tried to kill me."

"She couldn't have known it was you. All she saw was a wolf."

"You underestimate her, Roy. She knew. Oh, well she knew. Yes, she saw the body of a wolf, but what she tried to kill was the spirit of the woman who had taken her man."

He reached out and stroked the satiny black hair. "My poor Marcia. You were so close to dying."

Marcia's mouth tightened. "But now I am well and strong. At least the woman part of me. As for the other—it might be better if the silver bullet had struck a fraction lower and done its work completely."

Roy looked away.

"You know, do you not, what that woman stole from me with her silver bullet? She stole the power of the wolf, the freedom of the night. Do you remember, Roy, those nights when we ran wild and free? Do you remember the times together? The pleasures we gave each other? The pleasures we took?"

"I remember," he said. Still he did not look at her.

"Never again will I know that wild joy," she said. "Now in the night you must walk alone."

Roy faced her. He looked deep into the green eyes. "Is there no way—"

"None. The thing that happens to me now is my curse for as long as I live. I must bear those nights alone."

"Let me stay with you," Roy said.

"No. The change—I would rather die than have you see the thing I become. Now that my strength has returned, I can control it on most nights, but sometimes, when the moon is low and full, as it is tonight—" Marcia left the sentence unfinished.

Roy stroked the smooth, naked curve of her waist where it flowed into the lean hip. "I love you, Marcia. I would share anything with you."

"Not this," she snapped. Then her tone softened. "But you can share with me the vengeance against the woman who has destroyed half of me."

Roy nodded slowly. He would do whatever he must to keep this green-eyed woman.

Marcia looked over at the darkening curtain across the window. Outside, the daylight was falling. "If it were possible, we would leave tonight," she said, "but I cannot travel when the moon is full."

"Are you—can we be sure Karyn is still in Seattle?"

"She is still there," Marcia said. "The gypsies watch her for us. She can make no move that the gypsies do not see."

"Why do the gypsies do this for us?" Roy asked.

"Because they fear us. They know the power we have, and what we could do to them and their children if we wished. We have their help and their protection only because they fear the werewolf."

"I don't like to talk about it," Roy said.

Marcia's eyes were bright and mocking. "Oh, don't you? Tell me you don't like it when the night comes and you feel your body change. Tell me you don't like the taste of living flesh and raw hot blood."

Roy could not answer. The woman's words brought on an excitement that was almost sexual.

"Of course you like it," Marcia went on. "Out under the moon you glory in the power of the werewolf. You are unstoppable, invincible. No living thing can hurt you. Nothing can kill you.

Nothing, save the fire. . . . " In the dim light her teeth gleamed. "And silver."

It grew dark inside the trailer. Roy could barely make out the long, white shape of the woman lying among the cushions. Outside, the night had come. A pale glow beyond the green curtain signaled the rising moon. Roy felt its pull in the quickening of his senses and the uneasiness in his joints. His eyes were drawn toward the curtained window.

On the bed Marcia's body jerked in a sudden spasm. Her mouth twisted in pain.

"Leave me now," she said.

"Marcia, I—"

"Leave me!" The green eyes blazed with pain and pent-up fury.

Roy rose awkwardly to his feet. He stumbled to the door at the rear of the trailer. He pushed it open and stepped out into the cool night. As he closed the door he heard the rusty bolt scrape into place on the inside.

He turned toward the edge of the clearing where the moon was coming into view over the tops of the trees. To his sharpened senses the night held no secrets. He heard the scuttling of small creatures through the brush, and saw them darting among the shadows. The scents of the trees and the grasses and the night flowers were sharp in his nostrils.

The change from man to wolf, Roy had learned,

could come on any night. He could will himself
to change or, sometimes, prevent it. But on a night
like this, with the moon at its full power, the call
was impossible to resist.

Roy pulled at the collar of his shirt, letting the
cool night air flow in at his throat. He began to
walk toward the forest that rimmed the clearing.
He tore his shirt open, heedless of the flying buttons, and pulled it free of his belt. The muscles
jumped beneath his skin, his limbs twitched against
the growing ache in his joints. He stripped the
shirt from his back and let it fall to the grass. His
breath came in short, hot bursts. He began to run.

5

THE UPPER RIM OF the full moon edged above the tops of the Douglas firs on the hill to the east of Karyn Richter's home in Mountlake Terrace. Karyn stood at the French windows, watching it, her mind far away.

"How did it go with the doctor today?"

Startled, Karyn turned to see David standing in the room behind her.

"I didn't hear you come in," she said.

David Richter had a strong, clean-shaven face. He kept his graying hair short and neatly combed. He was in good physical condition, except for a slight bulge around the middle, and looked younger than his forty-eight years.

"Were you watching something out there?" he asked, nodding toward the window.

"No, just daydreaming." She gave a small, unconvincing laugh. "Can you daydream after dark?"

David smiled briefly, but his eyes remained serious.

Karyn shrugged. "Dr. Goetz said 'Come back next week.' Aside from that he didn't have much to say. No suggestions, no advice, just 'See you next week.' "

"Well, you look good, so he must be helping."

Karyn smiled at her husband. Dear, stolid, loyal David. In his heart he was surely convinced that her fears were the delusions of a borderline hysteric, but he would spring to her defense if any other man suggested as much. It was for David's sake as much as her own that she had to rid her mind of the horrible memories of Drago. For David, she would go on seeing Dr. Goetz or any other doctor he wanted, as long as there was a chance of getting better.

They both turned at a commotion in the next room, and six-year-old Joey Richter dashed in and skidded to a stop in front of them.

"Can I stay up and watch television?" the boy said hopefully, switching his gaze between Karyn and David. "It's Clint Eastwood," he added, as though this would influence the decision in his favor.

David looked to Karyn, signaling with his eyes that this one was up to her.

"What did Mrs. Jensen say?" Karyn asked.

The boy looked down at the scuffed toes of his tennis shoes. "She said no," he reported.

"Then it's no," Karyn said. "It's time for bed, and anyway, you've seen Clint Eastwood."

"I saw *Dirty Harry*," he explained patiently. "Tonight it's *Magnum Force*."

"To bed," Karyn said firmly.

"Oh, okay," Joey said, with all the martyrdom a six-year-old could muster. In another moment, though, the defeat was forgotten as he kissed first his father, then Karyn, good-night.

"Will you come up and tuck me in?" he asked, Karyn with his arms tight around her neck.

"I'll be up just as soon as Mrs. Jensen gets you ready," she promised.

At the sound of her name, Mrs. Jensen appeared in the doorway. To Karyn and David, she said, "He was trying to get you to let him stay up, I suppose."

"There was some mention of a Clint Eastwood movie," Karyn said.

Mrs. Jensen clucked her tongue in disapproval. "Always he wants to watch the shoot-'em-ups. Such trash. You couldn't force him to watch a nice wholesome Walt Disney."

"They're dumb," Joey complained. "Nobody ever shoots anybody."

"That's enough, Joey," David said, not unkindly. "Go along up with Mrs. Jensen now."

From a standing start the boy took off and dashed past the housekeeper and out the doorway. They could hear his small feet pounding up the stairs to his bedroom. Mrs. Jensen sighed and rolled her eyes in a long-suffering expression that did not hide her affection for the boy. She followed him out of the room.

David stretched and yawned. "I think I'll turn in early myself tonight. How about you?"

Karyn felt the tightening of her skin that always came when she thought about sex. The years of therapy had helped her considerably, but she still had problems.

She could never completely forget those last weeks with Roy, when he was going through the terrible change. She had not known at first what was happening to him, but found his touch suddenly repellent. Then after Drago, there was the crazy time with Chris Halloran. They had plunged into wild sex games, hoping to dull the remembered horror. Finally, inevitably, they had failed.

David Richter was a gentle, if unimaginative, lover. Sex with him had been satisfactory most of the time. Still, for Karyn, the residue of fear remained. Naturally, she had talked about it with David and with Dr. Goetz. They were both most reassuring and supportive, but there was always the worm of doubt.

She took David's hand and pressed it warmly. "I'm not really sleepy," she said. "I think I'll stay up and read for a while."

"Do you want me to get you a pill?"

Karyn did not miss the flicker of David's eyes as he glanced through the window at the rising moon. Normally he did not approve of her taking sleeping pills, but he knew how the full moon disturbed her.

"I don't think so," she said. "I haven't used a pill in months, and I'd just as soon stay away from them."

"Would you like to play a little backgammon? Give me a chance to win back some of my losses?"

Karyn smiled at him. She knew he was reluctant to leave her downstairs alone, and she loved him for it, but it was high time she made it clear that she was not an invalid.

"You go on to bed, dear," she said. "I know you have to be up early. I'll be along in a little while."

Mrs. Jensen reappeared in the doorway. "The young man is ready to be tucked in."

Karyn and David went up together to Joey's room at the head of the stairs. The wallpaper featured the exploits of Spiderman. It was chosen personally by Joey to replace what he called "those dumb ducks" that had decorated the walls when the room was a nursery.

Karyn smiled down at the boy and remembered how the idea of being a stepmother had worried her at first. When she was married to Roy, they had talked now and then about having children, but there was always a list of things they wanted to do first.

David Richter had become, unexpectedly, a father at forty-two. He treated the child with a kind of careful affection, as though afraid he might somehow damage the boy. Joey was three when his mother had died of cancer, and David had a couple of rough months trying to be both parents until he found Mrs. Jensen. Karyn was the first woman David had been seriously involved with since his wife's death, and he was delighted when she and Joey had hit it off.

The boy sat up in bed and hugged first his father, then Karyn. He lay down again while Karyn went through the nightly ritual of tucking the blankets close to his firm, wiry little body.

"G'night, Mom," the boy said. "G'night, Dad."

David and Karyn had spent considerable time discussing what Joey should call her after they were married, but the boy solved the problem for them immediately, figuring that if the blond lady was married to Dad, she was Mom, and that was that.

Leaving the door open a couple of inches, the way Joey liked it, Karyn and David stepped back into the hall. Karyn kissed her husband lightly.

"Go on to bed," she said. "I'll be in soon."

She went back downstairs and into the living room. A stack of magazines was spread across the coffee table. Karyn picked out this month's *Redbook* and carried it back into the family room. She could hear Mrs. Jensen's television set playing faintly in the housekeeper's room at the rear of the house. Karyn smiled at the distant popping of gunshots. Mrs. Jensen was watching *Magnum Force*.

For perhaps a quarter of an hour, Karyn tried but failed to focus her attention on the magazine. What she needed, Karyn decided, was something to really occupy her mind during the day. Something that would take enough effort to leave her honestly tired at bedtime. There was little for her to do around the house. Mrs. Jensen ran it with cool Scandinavian efficiency. Karyn was grateful for the help, but secretly wished that once in a while the housekeeper might leave something for her to do.

To help fill in the days, Karyn spent a few hours a week doing volunteer work at the Indian school. It was useful work, but also very "in" this season, and they had more volunteers up there now than Indians.

What she really wanted to do was to go back to work. Karyn had experience in working with conventions, and felt she could find some sort of related work with one of the large Seattle hotels. She could handle it now, physically and mentally,

Karyn was sure. David might not be enthusiastic, but if she really wanted to do it he would not stand in her way.

Finally she laid the magazine aside and stood up. She was still not sleepy, and did not want to go up and lie awake in bed, disturbing David. She wandered into the kitchen and took down the plastic spray bottle and long-nosed watering can she used for her plants. Karyn had an understanding with Mrs. Jensen that Karyn alone had responsibility for the plants. It pleased her to look after them—tiny living things which were hers alone, and which depended on her for their existence. After the sadistic slaughter of her little dog that summer by the creatures of Drago, Karyn would never again keep a pet. The plants were as close a substitute as she felt she could handle.

They grew in pots in an airy room at the side of the house. David liked to call it the sunroom. It amused Karyn, a Southern Californian, that any room in any house in Seattle should be called the *sun*room, but she never told that to David.

Karyn went first to the chlorophytum, the spider plant. The graceful green leaves, with their white stripes, arced like a fountain up and over the edge of their hanging pot. Karyn felt the soil with her finger and found it moist.

No drink for you today, she thought, just a nice little spray to perk you up. She pushed the plunger on the plastic bottle, and a fine mist of water dampened the leaves. Talking to plants, Karyn knew, was foolishness for addled old ladies. But it didn't count, she told herself, if you didn't do it out loud. At any rate, she stopped short of giving them personal names.

Her next stop was the Boston fern. She stood back a little and admired the buoyant arch of the fronds, their fine, lacy detail. She stepped closer and saw that a little spider had moved in and was busily spinning a web among the leaves. Karyn started to pinch the spider off in a piece of Kleenex, but stayed her hand in midair. You have a right to live too, she thought, and balled up the Kleenex and stuffed it into her pocket.

She always went to the philodendron last, because it was her personal favorite. It was a masculine plant, growing strong and glossy, climbing the moss-covered pole like an athlete. We'll soon need a bigger pot for you, my friend, Karyn thought. She gave the healthy leaves a light spray and added a touch of water and plant food to the soil, where the tough, sinewy roots drew their nourishment.

When she was finished Karyn stood back and smiled at her little garden. Then she took the spray bottle and watering can back to the kitchen. She went around the house, checking all the doors and windows, making sure they were all locked. She knew, of course, that Mrs. Jensen did that every night before she retired, but it made Karyn feel better to see to the locks herself. The last thing she did was draw the draperies across the French windows, shutting out the cold light of the full moon.

6

MOVING IN STRONG strides across the moon-bright clearing, Roy Beatty reached the edge of the forest. It was like coming home. He stripped off all his clothes and let them fall to the ground. Standing upright made him feel constricted, and he sank gratefully to his knees, leaning forward to dig his fingers into the soft earth. He stretched out full length and lay for a moment with his face pressed to the sweet-smelling carpet of moss and leaves. With a deep sigh he rolled onto his back. Above him, through the cross-hatching of branches, he could see the full moon riding high and cold. The rush of blood through his veins became a roaring in his ears.

A short, sharp pain stabbed into his forehead,

and he cried out. His body jerked over onto one side as though controlled by wires. He cramped into a curled, fetuslike position. As he lay there, the man's face stretched and distorted like modeling clay until all resemblance to Roy Beatty was lost. His nose and jaw thrust forward and became a muzzle. His ears grew longer and tapered themselves into blunt points. A series of convulsions seized his body. When the tremors quieted he stretched again, and new, powerful muscles moved under the skin. Where there had been bare flesh, thick fur, golden tan and glossy, now covered his body.

In minutes the change was complete. The creature that had been a man rose to its feet, unsteadily at first, then more confidently as it gathered strength. Braced on four sinewy legs, the beast pointed its muzzle to the night sky.

The wolf opened its throat and howled. A quavering cry that chilled the blood of the gypsies locked away in their trailers nearby. The wolf exulted in the renewed power of its body. It moved easily through the forest, picking up speed as it went. Finally it charged ahead at its full speed— faster than a man could run, faster than any natural wolf. It crashed heedlessly through the undergrowth, the thick coat of fur protecting its hide from thorns and broken ends of branches. The essence of the man that had been Roy Beatty shrank and retreated to a dark tiny corner of the

mind of the beast. All rational thought was wiped
out. There was only the raging hunger of the
werewolf.

The inhuman howling carried clearly to the
trailer where Marcia Lura was locked away from
the night. The thing on the floor scrambled over
to the door and pressed its face against the cool
metal. From the misshapen mouth came a sound—
something between a woman's sob and the growl
of a wolf.

Through the forest the huge pale wolf loped on.
Dimly remembered in the animal brain were those
other nights when the sleek black she-wolf ran at
his side. Then the way she looked, moving powerfully, gracefully, and her sharp female scent on
the night air, had driven the pale wolf half-mad
with animal lust. Three years before, on a night of
terror in the village of Drago, he had lost the
female forever.

On that night, as the fire consumed the village
and destroyed the others, the huge, pale wolf had
broken through the flames to where the female lay
wounded and dragged her to safety. The silver
bullet missed ending the dual life of the black wolf
and Marcia Lura by the breadth of a hair. Over
long agonized months, Roy Beatty had nursed the
woman back from near death. Now, at least in her
human form, the only mark of the wound she bore

was the silver-white streak through her midnight hair. As to the other——Roy could only imagine the things that happened to Marcia on the nights she locked herself away from him. He knew only that the lean, beautiful she-wolf would not return. That hunger would never be fed.

But there was the other hunger, the hunger that drove the werewolf endlessly through the night. The killing. The tearing away of living flesh, the crunch of bone between powerful jaws, the sweet-salty taste of warm blood.

As the werewolf reached the far side of the wood, it slowed and moved cautiously through the last of the trees. Roy Beatty had learned much in the three years since he went down under the slashing teeth of the she-wolf and awoke to find himself forever changed. He had learned to move with stealth and to kill with the smallest possible commotion.

The wolf checked abruptly as a change in the night breeze brought the scent of living prey. Moving crouched and silent through the shadows, he inched to the top of a grassy knoll that overlooked the moonlit meadow. The great yellow eyes searched out the quarry.

Along a rutted dirt road that wound through the pasture land walked a boy of about ten. He was headed toward the lights of a farmhouse a mile away where the highway skirted the fields.

The black lips of the werewolf twitched as the

boy scuffed along the road, whacking idly at tall weeds with a stick. The boy had short, reddish hair and a spattering of freckles across his face. He wore faded jeans and a light jacket. The scene stood out in sharp relief under the bright moon.

The muscles bunched in the wolf's haunches as the beast gathered itself for the attack. It would be over in seconds. Before the boy could cry out, the wolf would have him by the throat.

At the last possible instant, the wolf held back. The breeze carried a new scent that held him motionless. As he watched the boy, a shaggy white dog bounded up the road from the direction of the farmhouse, flapping its great brush of a tail happily.

The wolf crouched low again, its belly brushing the ground. Although the wind was in his favor, he saw the dog break off its playful romp around the boy, then brace stiffly, testing the air. The fur ruffed up on the back of the dog's neck as it felt the presence of danger. He barked a warning into the darkness.

It would, of course, be no contest. The dog did not live that could last two minutes against a werewolf. Still, there would be a delay in getting at the boy. The clamor might arouse someone in the house. The boy might escape and alarm the people with a story of seeing a huge, pale wolf.

The boy walked on, calling for the white dog to stop fooling around. The werewolf watched from the top of the knoll, its cruel teeth gleaming in the moonlight. With a last half-hearted bark at the night, the dog trotted after the boy.

Slowly the muscles of the wolf relaxed as the boy and the dog rounded a turn in the road and went out of sight. The wolf turned in a slow circle, sampling the air, sorting out the many night smells. Finding what it wanted, the beast loped off over the meadow, away from the lights of the farmhouse.

After a quarter of a mile the werewolf slowed. Straight ahead was its kill for this night. There a black and white Holstein cow stood methodically chewing her cud. Beside the cow, its gangly legs folded under, rested her calf.

Killing this defenseless creature would not bring to the werewolf the fierce, orgasmic joy that came from killing a human, but it would deaden the wolf's awful hunger. The wolf eased closer. The cow raised her head, listening to the rustle of grass behind her. He reflexes were far too dull for her to sense the danger.

Anger and frustration at losing the boy aroused the killing lust in the heart of the werewolf. He sprang at the calf, hitting the awkward creature as it was trying to rise. The terrified calf was knocked sprawling at the feet of its mother.

The cow mooed in fear, and lowered its head in an ineffectual attempt to defend its calf. The wolf merely turned to snarl at the cow, then returned to the business of killing.

While the cow stomped helplessly around, the

wolf clamped its fearsome jaws on the neck of the calf. The spine snapped like a dry branch and the struggling young animal went limp.

Under the sorrowful gaze of the mother the wolf fed on the tender flesh of the calf and drank its blood. With an occasional growl he kept the cow from coming too close.

When the wolf had eaten its fill, it used its teeth to crack away the ribcage. Almost gently the bloody muzzle pushed into the chest cavity and tore loose the still-warm heart.

With the bloody organ in its mouth, the wolf rose from its kill and loped away across the meadow toward the forest. The cow lowered its head and nuzzled the mangled carcass.

The moon was low over the far horizon when the werewolf returned to the gypsy camp. He crossed the clearing between the forest and the little cluster of trailers with the heart of the calf still in his mouth, stopping at the trailer where, hours before, Roy Beatty had left Marcia Lura. The wolf dropped the heart outside the door and stood for a moment, his head cocked, ears pricked, listening. Then he turned and moved back to the edge of the forest.

Minutes later, as the pale wolf lay out of sight in the underbrush, the bolt lock of the trailer door shot back and the door scraped open. The pale wolf heard, but made no move to approach as something snatched the heart of the calf inside and the door slammed shut again. The sounds that came from the trailer then made those gypsies who lay close enough to hear sweat cold in their beds.

Hours later, with the first light of dawn streaking the sky, Roy Beatty stretched his aching body, pulled on his clothes, and walked toward the trailer.

7

HE KNOCKED LIGHTLY at the door of the trailer. Inside, the bolt scraped back and in a moment the door opened. Marcia reached out her hands to him and helped him inside. Roy clung to her and felt some of the woman's strength flow into his exhausted body. He stepped back after a minute and looked at her. Somehow, after she had gone through one of the agonizing transformations, Marcia looked her most beautiful. The silver-streaked hair fell loose to her shoulders. Deep fires glowed in the green eyes. Roy's breath caught in his throat.

"Lie down, my lover," she said. "and let me make you comfortable."

He let her lead him to the bed. It was freshly

made with crisp linen, the quilted comforter turned back neatly. Roy sank into the bed and closed his eyes. Marcia's hand was cool and soft on his forehead. In a half-dream, he felt her undo the buttons and ease the clothes from his body. He lay naked on the clean sheet as Marcia sponged him with a cool, aromatic liquid. He felt his tensed muscles gradually relax as the vitality flowed back into his body. He opened his eyes and smiled at her.

"You make me feel reborn," he said.

"I'll give you some tea," she said, "and soon you will feel even better."

He reached up and touched the undercurve of her breast. She leaned forward, letting the warm, round weight settle in his palm. Roy shifted his position on the bed as he felt his desire rise for the woman.

"We don't need the tea," he said.

Marcia placed her hand over his and pressed his fingers against her erect nipple. "The tea will be good for you, my darling. It will restore your body and make you strong."

She leaned down and kissed him lightly on the mouth, then walked over to the compact butane stove where a kettle of water boiled. She poured the scalding water over a powdering of herbs in the bottom of a heavy cup. She added a few drops of a thick brown liquid, and a spicy-sweet aroma filled the trailer.

Roy well remembered the first time he had drunk

the wild, sweet brew. It was in the small house where Marcia had lived alone in the village of Drago. Afterward there had been sex more intense than anything he had known before. Throughout that afternoon and into the night he had made love to the green-eyed woman in ways he had never imagined. She had taken him with her to the extreme limits of his endurance, then with a final, crashing climax had left him utterly drained.

It was on that same night, as he walked through the forest to the house where Karyn waited, that the black she-wolf with the strange green eyes had run him down. As he lay helpless beneath the beast, the cruel teeth had bitten deep into his shoulder. Roy had been sure then he was going to die. His head was forced back, and he had not the strength to protect his throat. But then, incredibly, the wolf had pulled back and left him. He had staggered home in a daze. Soon he realized why he had been spared, and what it meant to survive the bite of a werewolf.

Marcia handed him the steaming cup. Roy inhaled deeply. The heady aroma made his eyes tear.

"Drink it down," she said softly.

Holding the cup in both hands, he drank the tea and felt the heat of it hit his stomach and radiate throughout his body. There was a soft singing in his ears.

Marcia rested her hand on his bare leg, letting

her fingers curl down across his inner thigh. "I have a surprise for you."

"Really?" he said, smiling.

Her lips curved. "In a little while, but first I have something to tell you."

"Yes?"

"We are leaving here."

"I know. As soon as you are ready to travel."

"I am ready now. We are leaving today."

He frowned. "So soon?"

"Soon? I have waited three years. I am as well now as I will ever be."

"But there are arrangements to make—transportation—a place to stay—"

"The arrangements are taken care of," Marcia said. "I have reservations for us on a flight to Seattle out of San Francisco this evening. There will be a room there waiting for us, not far from where your Karyn now lives."

Roy propped himself up on an elbow. "You did all this without talking to me about it?"

Her fingers moved again on his thigh, slid up between his legs. "I know you aren't interested in tiresome details."

"Just the same, you could have told me."

Marcia guided the cup of tea to his lips, and he drank. "You're not having doubts about what we have to do?"

"No. Only—"

The long supple fingers worked on him. "Don't

feel sorry for your Karyn. Remember, she was no wife to you, yet she gave herself freely to your supposed friend. Now she shares the bed of this man Richter. She has crippled me and cuckolded you. Now it is our turn."

Roy drank more of the powerful tea. Visions flashed through his mind of Karyn's slim, naked body convulsed with passion as some faceless man pounded into her.

"Yes," he whispered. "Our turn."

Marcia took the empty cup from his hand and placed it on the floor. She stood up and slipped the silky garment she was wearing off over her head. She let it fall to the floor and stood with her strong brown legs slightly apart, letting him eat her with his eyes. She came toward him slowly, her breasts swaying with each step.

Roy started to rise from the bed to meet her. She laid a hand on his shoulder and eased him back down. He lay back obediently, watching her. She moved his legs apart and knelt between them. Her head dipped forward and her hair brushed his thighs as her lips closed around him.

She made it last a full hour. Then, as they lay together and Roy dozed, voices outside the trailer roused them. Loud voices. Marcia pulled gently away from him and stood up, throwing a light robe over her shoulders. Roy, now fully awake, got up too. They went over and stood at the small window.

Marcia eased the green curtain aside enough for them to look out.

Outside, Ignacio, the leader of the gypsies, stood talking to a large, red-faced man. Sniffing nervously about their feet was a shaggy white dog.

"None of the people here would do a thing like that," Ignacio was saying. "I know them."

"Don't give me that crap," said the red-faced man. "There was a trail of blood from the spot where the calf was killed, leading right into your camp. People told me I was makin' a mistake letting gypsies stay on my property, but like a damn fool I didn't listen to 'em."

Ignacio's eyes flicked over toward the trailer where Roy and Marcia watched from behind the curtain. They glanced at each other, then returned their attention to the two men outside.

"I will ask among the people," Ignacio said. "If I find anyone here is responsible for this, he will be punished. Be sure of that."

"That calf was worth plenty," the farmer said.

"You can take the money the calf is worth out of the wages you pay us for working in your fields," Ignacio said.

"Well—" The farmer glowered around the motley collection of campers and trailers, as though trying to spot the culprit. "I guess that will be okay. But if this ever happens again—"

"I assure you it won't happen again."

"It sure as hell better not," said the farmer, "or next time I bring the sheriff with me."

He started to walk away, but turned back as though he were not yet satisfied. "It's bad enough to lose the calf, but the way it was done—Jesus. All ripped apart. What kind of a man would kill an animal that way?"

Ignacio had no answer, and the farmer clumped off toward the trail that led through the woods. At the edge of the trees he turned and whistled sharply. The dog broke off its investigation of the trailers and followed the man.

Ignacio remained standing where he was. He turned his head and stared long at the trailer where Marcia and Roy stood watching.

"He knows," Roy whispered.

"Of course he knows," said Marcia, "but he would never dare to act against us."

"Maybe not, but we shouldn't push him too far. I'll go out and tell him we're leaving."

"As you wish," Marcia said indifferently. "I'll gather the things we will want to take with us."

When Roy dressed and went out, he found Ignacio sitting on the rear step of the camper where he lived with his wife and small daughter. The gypsy's face darkened as Roy approached.

Roy spoke awkwardly. "Ignacio, I—I wanted to tell you we are leaving."

"Leaving?" The gypsy could not keep the eagerness out of his voice. "For good?"

"Yes. You've been very kind letting us stay with you while Marcia was—ill. I'm grateful."

"You owe me nothing."

"She is better now, so we'll be on our way."

Ignacio nodded gravely. He offered no words of regret at their leaving. Roy knew well why they had been allowed to stay, and Ignacio was not a man to waste false words of farewell.

"Goodbye," Roy said.

The gypsy studied him, the black eyes nearly hidden beneath the tangled brows.

"God help you," he said.

8

KARYN STEPPED OUT of the elevator in the Seattle Sheraton Hotel, feeling highly pleased with herself. She had a job. At least she would have, starting next month—coordinating the new hotel's banquet facilities. It would be good to feel useful again.

Over the past several weeks there had been several discussions with David, who did not fully approve of her going back to work. Finally, though, he said he would not object if that was what she really wanted. Dr. Goetz thought it was a good idea, and he had helped convince David. She had arranged to work only twenty hours a week, and would have afternoons and evenings free for her family.

This morning she had been so excited about the job interview that she skipped breakfast. Now she was hungry. The hotel's coffee shop opened off the lobby, and Karyn went in. It was eleven o'clock, in between coffee-breakers and the lunch crowd, so the room was nearly empty. Karyn took a table near the window and ordered shrimp salad, boysenberry pie, and coffee. As she waited for the waitress to come back with the order, Karyn began to feel uneasy. At first it was nothing she could define, just a prickling of the skin and a sort of chill down her back. Then she knew what it was. Someone was watching her.

Karyn tried to shrug off the feeling. It was nerves, of course. The excitement of getting a job. Just sit still, she thought, and it will go away.

But it did not go away. Instead, the feeling of being watched grew stronger and more oppressive. The waitress brought her food and gave her an odd look.

Even though Karyn knew it was foolishness, the desire to turn around became too strong to resist. As casually as she could manage, Karyn turned in her chair and surveyed one by one the other customers. There was a haggard young mother trying to keep a pair of little boys in their chairs. A young man with an Army haircut, probably from Fort Lewis. An old man in a black mohair suit, reading a Hebrew newspaper. A woman with dark hair streaked with silver, studying the menu through oversized sunglasses. A fat woman cheating on her diet with a double caramel sundae. A young woman in a beautician's smock, with the name of the hotel stitched over the pocket.

That was all. An ordinary lot. And none of them watching her. At least, no one was watching when she turned to look.

Karyn returned to her food, but found she was no longer hungry. She knew she had to stop these imaginings. Be logical about it, she told herself. *Why* would anyone watch her? What reason could they have?

She snapped upright in the chair. Why would anyone wear dark sunglasses on a cloudy day?

Karyn turned again, quickly this time. Everything was as before—all the same customers sitting where they had been. All, except the dark-haired woman in the sunglasses. She was gone.

What had the woman looked like? Karyn bit her lip and tried to remember. The woman's eyes had been invisible behind the dark lenses, and the lower part of her face was hidden behind the menu. Deliberately? The only feature Karyn could recall was the startling slash of white through the blue-black hair. And yet the woman seemed familiar.

Karyn shook her head, impatient with herself. This was getting her nowhere. There was no earthly reason for anyone to be watching her. She had to stop these fancies. She resolved to tell Dr. Goetz about it. In his gentle, professional way he could settle her down, explain these irrational feelings.

She paid for her uneaten lunch and left the coffee shop. Outside the day had darkened as the heavy clouds pressed down on the city. There was nothing for Karyn to do at home, and she did not want to spend the day alone in the big house with only Mrs. Jensen for company.

She stood indecisively in front of the hotel and looked up and down the street. The marquee of a theater down the block advertised a movie she had been wanting to see. On an impulse she turned and walked to the theater, bought a ticket, and went in.

The audience was small for the early show, and Karyn found a seat by herself halfway down and on the aisle. She settled down to watch the movie, but soon began to shift uncomfortably in her seat. The feeling of being watched came back. It was stronger here in the darkened theater than it had been in the coffee shop.

Making no attempt this time to be casual, Karyn turned to scan the faces in the reflected light from the screen. No one was looking at her. She did not see the woman with the streak in her hair.

After that she found she could not concentrate on the movie, and soon left the theater. Outside, a light, dismal rain had begun. Karyn hurried the two blocks to the parking lot where she had left her car. Once she stopped and turned suddenly. She caught a fleeting impression of a woman half a block behind her, on the same side of the street. Just as Karyn turned the woman slipped into the entrance of a building. In the brief glimpse, all that Karyn could be sure of was that the woman was tall and dark. She walked slowly the rest of the way, turning several times to look behind her, but the woman did not reappear.

The Evergreen Motel was a neglected, U-shaped stucco complex at the northern city limits of Seattle. The Evergreen had no swimming pool, no television in the rooms, no automobile club recommendations, but it was private and cheap and did good Friday-night business among romantic couples from near-by offices. The couple in Room 9, however, had their minds on other things.

"Are you sure she didn't recognize you?" Roy Beatty asked.

"She never got a good look at my face," Marcia said. She smiled, the green eyes glowing with some deep emotion. "But I touched something in her memory. I let her see me twice, and I know she felt the beginnings of fear."

"Do you think that's a good idea?" Roy said. "Dragging it out like this?"

"My love, that *is* the idea. For what that woman did to me, and to you too, we want her to suffer. She must have time to worry about it."

Marcia lay back across the bed, stretching her long body sensuously. Roy did not look at her. He paced the worn carpet nervously.

"What do we do now?" he asked.

"Don't worry, darling, I have it all planned. I will let her see me again—just a glimpse here and there. Maybe we'll give her a quick look at you. That would give her something to think about. I have watched her at home, and I have a little something in mind there too. The important thing is to have patience. I want your Karyn to finally understand what is happening to her, and why, just before—" She left the unfinished sentence hanging.

"Before what?" Roy said.

Marcia sat up suddenly and swung around to face him. "Don't be stupid, Roy. You know what we have to do."

"Kill her, Marcia? Do we have to kill her? What good will that do?"

Marcia swung her long legs from the bed and walked over to stand in front of him. She looked deep into his eyes, holding her body close to his. Her voice was soft and carressing.

"It will give me peace, darling, after months of agony. It is something I must do. If you don't want to be a part of it, I will understand. Leave now if that's the way you feel, and I will go on alone."

Roy held himself away from the green-eyed woman for a moment, then put his hands on her shoulders and pulled her tight against him. He stroked her hair, gently fingering the streak of silver as though it were a wound. The gentle scent of sandalwood brought to his mind the intoxicating days and nights when they had first been together.

"I can't leave you," he said. "Whatever has to be done, we will do together."

"My Roy," she breathed close to his ear. "My lover." Gently she pulled him toward the bed.

"What did Dr. Goetz say?"

David Richter held his wife's hand and studied her worriedly.

"He said it was all in my head."

David frowned.

"I'm only kidding. He didn't say that in so many words, but that was the gist of his message. What he said was something like, 'Many people go through periods of mild paranoia. Even people with no other neuroses. For someone with your history, it isn't at all unusual. Nothing to worry about.' "

David squeezed Karyn's hand and nodded sagely. "I'm sure Dr. Goetz knows what he's talking about, dear."

"Not in this case, he doesn't," Karyn said. "There is someone following me. A woman. Since the other day when I first saw her in the coffee shop, I've seen her again on the street, once at the library, and again just this morning in a taxi driving by right in front of our house."

"You're sure it was the same woman?"

"I'm positive. She was dressed differently, and always had her face covered or turned away, but I couldn't miss that white streak in her black hair."

David listened thoughtfully. When Karyn finished speaking he rubbed his jaw and gazed off at a corner of the ceiling. "Karyn, about your going to work—do you think we might be rushing things a bit?"

"No, I don't! And what the hell does that have to do with anything?"

"I just thought that, well, the added strain of taking on an outside job just now might—might—"

"Might make me start imagining things?" Karyn finished for him. "Like people following me?"

"I didn't mean that exactly."

"Like hell you didn't." Karyn saw the hurt look come into his eyes, and she reached up to touch his cheek. "I'm sorry, David. I know you're trying to do what you think is best for me. So is Dr. Goetz. It's just that neither of you wants to consider the possibility that I am seeing exactly what I think I am seeing."

David smiled at her, but the doubt was still in his eyes. "I'm trying, dear. I'm really trying."

They talked no more about it that evening, and

went up to bed early. David fell asleep almost immediately. It was another hour before Karyn began to get drowsy. Then she was jolted back to full wakefulness. Something was moving around downstairs.

It was not any distinct sound that she could identify. Just a sort of soft shuffling. Then nothing. For a long time Karyn lay tense, staring into the darkness. She fought to convince herself that she had heard no sound, and she prayed that it would not come again.

Then she heard it again. Just the suggestion of movement. She wanted it to be Mrs. Jensen, but knew that it was not. The housekeeper moved with a firm, heavy tread, not the furtive shuffling Karyn heard now.

Her mind groped for possible explanations. The wind. The house settling. Mice. The plumbing. But it was no good. She knew it was none of these. She lay utterly still and listened. For many minutes the only sound was David's deep, regular breathing. Her ears ached with the effort of listening. Then it came again. Something sliding, like cloth on cloth. Then a muffled thump, barely audible, but unmistakably real.

"*David.*" Her voice was a rasping whisper.

"Wha—"

She placed her fingers lightly on his lips to silence

him as he awoke. When his eyes were fully open and alert, she took her hand away.

"What is it?" he said, whispering in reaction to her tension.

"There's something downstairs."

"What do you mean?"

"Sssh. Listen."

They sat up in bed, their shoulders touching, and listened. The seconds ticked by. Karyn's chest began to ache, and she realized she was holding her breath. She let it out in a long, silent sigh.

"I don't hear anything," David said. A touch of annoyance had crept into his voice.

"No, I heard something. Really."

For another interminable two minutes they sat in the bed, their heads cocked toward the door.

Nothing.

"Karyn—" David began, speaking now in a natural voice.

"I didn't imagine it," she said. "There's something down there. Or at least there was."

"Why do you say 'something' instead of 'someone'?"

"God, I don't know. What difference does it make?"

With a sigh, David threw back the covers. "I'll go down and look around."

Karyn watched as he got out of bed, pulled on a robe over his white pajamas, and went out into the hallway. She felt foolish. Like some giddy wife in an old television sitcom. *"Ricky, get up, I heard a burglar!" "Aw, go back to sleep, Lucy, ees nothing."*

Briskly she threw off the blankets and got up. At least she did not have to stay up here cowering in bed, playing out her role. Pulling on a quilted robe, she went out the door and headed down the hallway toward the stairs. At the head of the stairs she stopped to look into Joey's room. The boy was sleeping peacefully. Karyn went on down to join her husband.

All the lights were blazing now as David flicked them on as he walked from room to room. When Karyn reached the bottom of the stairs he was just coming back from the rear of the house. Behind him was Mrs. Jensen, her face puffy from sleep, her hair twisted around plastic rollers.

"Nothing down here," David said. Karyn knew he was making an effort not to let his irritation show.

"Mrs. Jensen," she said, "did you hear anything?"

"Not me. Not until Mr. Richter knocked on my door. But then, I sleep like the dead anyway."

Karyn looked around helplessly. "I'm sure I heard a noise down here."

"Well, there's nothing here now," David said. "You can go back to bed, Mrs. Jensen. Sorry to disturb you."

Karyn waited while David went around turning off the lights, then followed him upstairs. They got into bed and he lay rigidly with his back to her. She wanted to reach out and touch him, bring him close, but she could not. She had to listen. But there were no more sounds from downstairs. After a very long time she fell into a troubled sleep.

9

FOR THE NEXT TWO nights, Karyn slept fitfully. She was waiting, straining to hear even the smallest sound from downstairs that did not belong. All she heard were the normal creaks and snaps a house makes as it cools off at night, but her imagination gave them strange and sinister implications.

During the daytime she stayed close to the house. When she walked even as far as the mailbox she watched carefully behind her. No one followed.

Finally she began to relax a little. Maybe, just maybe, she *had* imagined those things—the watcher, the night sounds downstairs. Maybe everything was going to be all right.

Then her plants began to sicken.

The Boston fern was the first to show symptoms

of trouble. While making her rounds with the watering can and spray bottle, Karyn noticed several of the little saw-toothed fronds, curled and brown, lying on the floor under the fern. When she examined the plant more closely she found dying fronds, and the remaining, living fronds had lost their resiliency. She moved on to the spider plant and saw that the bladelike leaves no longer held their proud arch. The pointed tips on several were beginning to turn brown. Her pet, the philodendron, seemed robust still, but even its leaves looked duller than they should be.

Karyn heard Mrs. Jensen out in the kitchen. She called to her, and the housekeeper came out wiping her hands on a towel.

"Yes, Mrs. Richter?"

"Have you been watering the plants?"

"I never touch those plants. You asked me not to, as I remember."

"Yes, that's right. Thank you."

"Is that all?"

"Yes, that's all."

Karyn read the woman's resentment in the set of her shoulders as she marched back to the kitchen. She'd make it up to the housekeeper later, by praising the dinner or something.

Karyn walked around and looked at the plants again. There was no doubt that something was wrong with them. Even the strong philodendron. The trouble was that sick plants looked the same whether they were overwatered, underwatered, or suffering from any number of horticultural maladies. Karyn had always been careful about the watering, and she had seen to it that each got its proper amount of light and was kept within the acceptable temperature range. The soil had been specially blended at the store where she bought the plants; the nutrients she added at specified intervals came from there too.

She had heard the theory that plants can pick up the psychological vibrations of their people, and react to them, but she considered the idea ridiculous. All the same, something was definitely wrong with her plants, and Karyn resolved to watch them closely.

In the next 24 hours they got much worse. By then there was a generous scattering of dead brown fronds under the fern. The spider plant drooped sadly, its leaves turning yellow and curling in on themselves. The philodendron had completely lost its glossy good health. The leaves had paled and hung limp from the vine. The whole plant sagged against the post as though it were an effort to remain upright.

Karyn decided to wait no longer. She carried the three plants out to her little Datsun and drove off for Plant World on Aurora, where she had bought them. She felt just a little foolish rushing them off like sick children, but they *were* her responsibility.

She pulled into the parking lot at Plant World

and carried them in one by one. She was relieved to find an understanding woman at the counter, and not some smartass who would have to make jokes.

"My, they do seem to be feeling poorly, don't they?" the woman said.

"It just happened in the last couple of days," Karyn said. "What do you think is wrong with them?"

"I'd hate to take a guess. Mr. Bjorklund will be back this afternoon. He's awfully good with sick little fellows like these."

"Would it be all right if I left them here? I could come back tomorrow and talk to Mr.—"

"Bjorklund," the woman supplied. "Of course you can leave them, dear. Don't worry about them. I'll see to it they're made comfortable, and I'll watch over them until Mr. Bjorklund comes."

"Thank you," Karyn said. She resisted an impulse to give each of the sick plants a reassuring pat, and left the store.

A sense of depression came over her as she drove back home. The car seemed empty. She reminded herself sternly that it was just three plants she had left behind, not three children. To get out of the mood, she decided to stop in at the new Kenmore Shopping Mall and look around.

It was one of the new breed of two-level shopping centers, roofed over against the elements, and with an adjoining parking structure. Inside, the mall had bubbling fountains, potted shrubbery, and plastic park benches. The air had a scent of aerosol springtime. Soft, soothing music flowed from concealed speakers.

Karyn strolled slowly along, window-shopping the jewelry and clothing stores. She went into a leather goods shop and began to feel better, enjoying the tangy smell and tough-smooth feel of the merchandise.

She picked out a key case she thought David would like, and paid for it with her Master Charge card. While the clerk filled out the receipt she remembered that her parents had a wedding anniversary coming up soon. She left the leather shop with her purchase and stepped on the Down escalator to reach a gift shop on the lower level.

As she rode down on the silent moving stairway, Karyn glanced up at the overhead ledge. Just before she was carried underneath, she saw the face of Roy Beatty.

Her knees started to give way, and she clutched the black rubber handrail for support. The woman in front of her turned around and gave Karyn a look of disapproval.

When the escalator reached the bottom Karyn almost fell as her feet slid over the grate where the steps disappeared. The people coming off behind Karyn jostled her as she stood motionless, staring upward toward the ledge that was out of sight now.

After a moment, she took hold of herself and hurried across the mall to where the matching escalator carried people up. She got on and climbed the moving steps, ignoring the irritated looks she got from the shoppers she pushed past.

Once back on the upper level she had to look around for a moment to get her bearings. She located the ledge with the railing overlooking the Down escalator, where she had seen Roy. The only people there now were two young boys, who leaned over to watch the moving row of people slide down and out of sight. There was no sign of Roy Beatty, or anyone who looked like him.

Karyn hurried over and spoke to the boys. "What happened to the man who was standing here?"

The boys looked at each other, then back at Karyn. "What man?"

"He was standing right here where you are now. He was looking down."

"There wasn't any man here that we saw." The boys started to edge away from her.

Karyn started to insist that there certainly had been a man standing right here not three minutes ago, then she stopped, realizing how foolish it would be to argue with the children. In frustration she spun around, her eyes ranging over the people who moved among the shops.

She saw him again just as he vanished down one of the broad aisles leading to an exit. He wore a denim jacket and faded jeans. The hair was longer than Roy had worn his, but it was the same shade of pale tan, and the broad shoulders brought Karyn a pang of memory. She left the two boys staring after her and followed the man.

She reached the exit and saw that it opened on a concrete walkway across to the parking structure. No one was on the bridge. Karyn hurried across and peered around among the parked cars. There was no sign of the man in denim. Karyn looked down and saw her hands were shaking. She leaned for a moment against one of the thick pillars for support. Somewhere she had dropped the package with David's key case, but she did not go back to look for it.

Dr. Goetz sat facing her in one of his chrome and leather chairs. He wore a professional, concerned expression.

"I feel a little silly," Karyn said, "calling you from the shopping center as though it were some kind of life-or-death emergency. All the same, I'm glad you could see me."

The doctor smiled gently. "I hate to say, 'That's what I'm here for,' because it sounds so Marcus Welby. But that's what I'm here for, Karyn."

"Now that I'm here, I don't know where to start."

"Tell me about the man you saw at the shopping mall. Did you get a good look at him?"

"Yes. It was just for a second or two, but I saw him very clearly. Then the escalator took me down under the ledge where he was standing."

"Did he say anything to you?"

"No."

"Make any gesture? Any sign that he knew you?"

"He just looked at me."

"And you say he resembled your former husband."

"Dr. Goetz, he *was* my former husband. That man was Roy Beatty."

Dr. Goetz squeezed his lower lip thoughtfully between thumb and forefinger. After several seconds he spoke. "As I recall, you told me Roy Beatty died three years ago."

Karyn felt the beginnings of a headache. She said, "I don't *know* that he died in the Drago fire. I assumed that he did. Obviously, I was wrong. If I saw him in the Kenmore Mall this morning, then he's alive."

Dr. Goetz got out of his chair and came over to sit beside her on the sofa. His pale blue eyes searched her face, then became unreadable. "Karyn, I think maybe we were hasty in cutting you down to one visit a week. If it's possible, I'd like to see you more often. Twice. Three times, if you could manage it."

Karyn wanted to cry. Ever since the crack-up in

Las Vegas, she had made steady progress in her therapy. Until now. What was happening to her? She knew how it must sound—someone following her, noises in the night, and now seeing her supposedly dead husband. The classic symptoms of paranoid schizophrenia.

For the first time in many months Karyn wondered if she might be losing her grip on reality. Maybe she did need more time with the analyst.

"I'll talk to my husband about it," she said. "Goodbye, Doctor."

The front door of the Richter house flew open and banged shut with an unnecessary slam. Joey Richter raced in, dumped his schoolbooks on the hall table without slowing down, and made a speedy circuit of the downstairs rooms. He came to a stop at the foot of the stairs.

"Mom!" he called

Mrs. Jensen came down the stairs carrying a basket of laundry. "Your mother isn't home. And if she was, she'd tell you not to slam the door."

"Where is she?"

"She had an appointment downtown."

"With the doctor?"

"I wouldn't know."

"Why did she have to see the doctor today? This isn't her day."

"I'm sure I couldn't say."

"She's probably having those dreams again. The ones that scare her."

"I don't know anything about any dreams," Mrs. Jensen said. "Now come in and eat your lunch. It's good vegetable soup."

"Campbell's?"

"No, it's homemade."

"I like Campbell's."

"You're going to like this even better. Come on and I'll dish it up for you."

Joey clumped into the kitchen and ate two bowls of the soup, which he admitted was almost as good as Campbell's. He finished up with a peanut butter and jelly sandwich and a glass of milk while Mrs. Jensen loaded clothes into the washer in the adjoining laundry room.

"I wish Mom would get home," Joey said. "I want to tell her about the face last night."

Mrs. Jensen came back into the kitchen. "Did you say a face?"

"Yeah. Last night it looked right in my window. Wow, was it ugly!"

"You had a dream, you mean."

"Nah, it wasn't any dream, it was a face. All kind of scrunched up and hairy and with great big teeth. Really ugly."

The housekeeper studied the boy for a moment. "Did it scare you?"

Joey met her eye seriously, then broke into mischievous laughter. "No way. I knew who it was all the time."

"Who?"

"That crazy Kelly in a rubber mask. He's always doing crazy things. Probably climbed up on the roof and thought he could scare me. Crazy."

"What would he be doing up so late?" Mrs. Jensen said with stern disapproval.

"He gets to stay up as late as he wants to," Joey said. "I'm as old as he is and don't even get to stay up and watch '*Kojak*.' "

"It does you a lot more good to get your sleep than staying up to watch junk like that. Or playing dumb tricks like your friend Kelly."

"I'll tell Mom," Joey said. "She'll buy me a mask, a horribler one than Kelly's even, then I'll go to his house and *really* scare him."

"I don't think you'd better tell your mother about it," Mrs. Jensen said.

"Why not? She'll buy me a mask. I know she will."

"Maybe so, but your mother's not been feeling too well, and I don't think it would do her any good to hear about faces at the window and such foolishness."

"Awww."

"You want her to get well, don't you?"

"Sure."

"Then don't go bothering her with this kind of stuff."

"Oh, okay."

Joey jumped up from the table and ran outside, slamming the door firmly. Mrs. Jensen looked after him with a worried frown, then shook off the thought and got busy picking up the dishes.

10

ROOM 9 IN THE Evergreen Motel was cool and dim in the pale light that filtered in through the curtains. Roy Beatty sat beside the bed, holding the hand of the woman who lay among the twisted sheets.

"I was worried when you didn't come home last night," he said.

Marcia rolled her head on the pillow and looked at him. There were shadows around her deep green eyes, but they shone as brilliantly as ever.

She said, "I'm all right now. It was frightening when it happened. Last night was the first time I wasn't prepared for it. It must have been the excitement of being so close, of seeing at last what we are going to do. I could not control the change."

Roy stroked a strand of black hair from her forehead. "My poor Marcia."

"It doesn't matter," she said. "There is a patch of trees near their house. I was able to reach them and stay there until daylight. No one saw me, except perhaps the boy, and I don't think he knew what he was seeing."

"Maybe we should forget about this. Go away from here. For your sake."

"Forget about it?" Marcia sat straight up in bed, and it seemed to Roy that he could see the strength flow into her body. "Never! I have not waited this long, come this far, only to turn back. As for what happened to me last night, I will take care to see that it does not happen again. I will keep a tighter hold on my emotions."

Roy sighed and nodded his head slowly. He stood up and walked over to the window where he pulled aside the curtain and looked out over the asphalt of the parking lot. The Evergreen was not on one of the main highways which ran through Seattle, and in the middle of the week there was little business. There were only three cars parked outside, the white Ford which Roy had rented, and two others. They looked cold and abandoned in the misting rain.

"If it's going to rain, I wish to Christ it would really rain," he said irritably. "This everlasting drizzle is driving me up the wall."

"We won't have to be here much longer," Marcia

said. "Your Karyn is frightened and worried now. The way we want her."

"Why do you keep calling her *my* Karyn?"

"I'm sorry. It was just an expression. I won't do it any more if it annoys you."

"Well, it does. Anyway, what's the need for all this?" Roy continued to stare out the window. "Why don't we do what we came to do and get it over with?"

Marcia slipped out of bed and came over to stand beside him. She took his broad hand in hers and held it against her smooth, naked hip. "Indulge me in this, my Roy, and I will make it up to you."

He held himself tensely, not looking at her. She moved his hand across the flat of her stomach and down to the crisp bush of pubic hair. He resisted for a moment more, then surrendered and turned to face her. He whispered her name. His fingers probed between her legs and found the dampness there.

Marcia grasped his wrist and held it, keeping his hand pressed against her. "When this business is over I will make you very happy. I know I have not been a complete woman to you these past months, but I will make it right in a hundred ways. You will never regret being with me, darling." She drew back and her eyes searched his face. "You *are* with me, aren't you, my Roy?"

"You know I am."

"Good." She kissed him lightly on the mouth,

then slipped away and began to put on her clothes. Once again she was businesslike.

"Are you sure you were seen at the shopping center?"

"Karyn saw me, all right," he said. "Once when she rode the escalator below where I was standing, and again as I was going out. She followed me to the parking lot, but I lost her there."

"Good. She will have much to think about, many things to remember when we take the next step."

"And that is—"

"We kill the boy."

Roy drew in his breath and let it out slowly. "Is that the only way?"

"It is the best way. It is the way that will hurt her the most before we finally finish with her." Marcia fixed him with her eyes. "Do you have some objection?"

"It's just—killing the boy—"

Marcia's laugh clattered off the walls in the small room. "Come now, Roy. After the things you have done these past three years? The blood you have spilled? Would one more killing bother you?"

He could not meet her eye. "Remember, Marcia, I wasn't born to this life the way you were. What I am, you made me. I am not all wolf. I still have human emotions sometimes."

Marcia stepped close to him and touched his face. "I understand, my darling. The time will come when you will no longer be held back by remorse.

Until then you will take strength from me. I know that when the time comes to act, you will not fail."

"When—will it be time?"

"From now on we will watch the house every night. The first time they leave the boy alone, you will kill him."

11

MR. BJORKLUND SHRUGGED and spread his hands in a gesture of helplessness. "I'm sorry," he said.

Karyn waited for a moment for him to say something more. When he didn't she looked down at the long wooden counter between them. There, each in its familiar pot, were her three plants. They were barely recognizable. The fern and the spider plant were yellow-brown, shriveled, and ugly, dead, ropy things that had nothing to do with the vibrant living greenery they had been. Only the tough philodendron had not given up. With the tenacity of the dying it clung to the mossy post, but its leaves were pale and sickly, splotched with brown like the hands of old people with liver spots.

"I'm afraid they're goners," Mr. Bjorklund said. "There was nothing I could do."

"Thanks, anyway," Karyn said dully.

"What have you been feeding them?"

Karyn looked up at him curiously. "I didn't feed them anything, except what you gave me. I kept them in the soil you blended for me, and I was very careful about watering them."

"Somebody fed them," the nurseryman said. "They've been poisoned."

Karyn stared at him.

"I ran a test on the soil in all three pots. Each one is saturated with enough herbicide to kill a Douglas fir."

"That isn't possible."

Bjorklund shrugged again. "All I can tell you is what the tests showed."

"Is there some way the herbicide could have got into the soil accidentally?"

"Nope. It was added to the soil deliberately and carefully. The concentration was heaviest right down around the roots. Then way I figure it, somebody jammed the nozzle of a plastic squeeze bottle down in there and pumped the stuff in."

"Why would anybody want to do that?"

"You tell me."

Karyn looked down again at the sorry shriveled things that had been her plants. "Then they're all—dead?"

"As last winter's corsage," he said. "The philodendron might hang on for a while if we transplant it into some rich new soil and feed it special nutrients, but if you want my opinion, it's a goner too. I'll try to save it if you want me to."

"No," Karyn said abruptly. "No, never mind." She turned and started for the door.

"How about replacements?" Bjorkland called after her. "I can fix you up with three nice healthy plants."

"No, thank you."

"What about these pots? They're yours."

"You keep them," Karyn said without looking back. "I have no more use for them."

The house in Mountlake Terrace seemed painfully empty. Karyn wandered around restlessly, then stopped short as she realized she was avoiding the family room. That was where her plants had been.

For God's sake, they were only vegetables! she reminded herself. And yet she had to admit now that they had come to mean much more to her. Far too much.

She saw the absurdity of her feelings, but seeing it did nothing to lessen her sense of loss. The plants had been hers, and hers alone, and now they were dead. Murdered, if it was accurate to say a plant had been murdered. Who would do a thing like that? And why? It had to be someone who was trying to get at her. The someone who was in her house the other night?

She put aside the suspicions forming in her mind when David came home. She told him briefly that her plants had died, without going into details. There was no way to tell him without sounding more paranoid than ever.

David was very kind. Sensing her mood, he put an arm around her and patted her gently. "You know something, we haven't been out together for a long time," he said. "What do you say we have dinner tonight at Teagle's?"

"But you have to work tomorrow."

"So I'll go in a little late. The business will hold together. How about it?"

"I'd like it," Karyn said. "Very much."

David gave her hand a squeeze. "It will be good for you to get out of the house."

Mrs. Jensen came in and cleared her throat to get their attention. "Will you be wanting an early dinner tonight?" she said.

"We're going out," David told her. "Just make something for Joey."

The housekeeper nodded and turned to leave.

"Oh, Mrs. Jensen," David called her back.

"Yes?"

"There was a ladder left leaning up against the back of the house the other day. I had to put it away."

Karyn looked up quickly. "A ladder?"

Mrs. Jensen made a clucking sound with her tongue. "Ah, that would have been one of Joey's little friends. The Kelly boy."

"I wish Joey would tell his friends to leave things in the garage alone. Or at least put them back when they're finished."

"I'll speak to him about it," said Mrs. Jensen.

It was warm in the house, but Karyn caught herself shivering as though she were caught in a cold draft.

12

AT FIRST THE IDEA of getting dressed and going out had seemed hardly worth the trouble to Karyn. It could not change anything. Still, it was sweet of David to make the effort to please her, so she went along with it. However, as she sat before her dressing table applying a touch of pale pink lipstick, she found she was truly looking forward to a night out. As David said, it *had* been a long time.

She stood up and looked herself over in the full-length mirror on the closet door. The long dress clung nicely, flattering her trim figure. Not bad, she decided, for a neurotic lady closing in on thirty. She added a final dab of perfume and went downstairs to where David was waiting.

Mrs. Jensen went to the front door with them as they left.

"We may be home late," David said. He turned to smile at Karyn. "We might decide to go out dancing somewhere after dinner."

Karyn returned his smile.

"I won't wait up, then," Mrs. Jensen said.

"You'll see that Joey gets to bed on time?" Karyn said.

Mrs. Jensen gave her a brief smile that said she had been taking care of Joey before Karyn got there, and could handle it very well now, thank you.

David gave Karyn his arm, and they followed the flagstone walk around to the garage. Halfway there, Karyn pulled up. Had she seen something move in that white Ford parked up the block? Whose car was that, anyway. She was sure it did not belong to any of the neighbors.

"Is something wrong?" David said.

"Nooo," she said slowly. Then more emphatically. "No. I just caught my heel on the edge of the stone. Let's go."

There was nothing moving in the white car now. Probably she had imagined it. The Ford most likely belonged to someone visiting the neighbors. No point in mentioning it to David and getting their evening off to an uncomfortable start.

Mrs. Jensen watched from the doorway as the Richters drove off. It was high time they had an evening out together, she thought. Much of the time she felt Mr. Richter worked too hard. And Mrs. Richter, well, she had her own problems. She closed the door and went inside.

She let Joey stay up to watch "Charlie's Angels," which he said he enjoyed because of the pretty girls. Mrs. Jensen left him to enjoy the girls alone while she went to her own room to watch an old Bette Davis movie on another channel. At ten o'clock she sent Joey up to bed, ignoring his pleas to watch "Baretta." When the boy was tucked in, Mrs. Jensen resumed watching her movie on the larger set in the Richters' family room.

The movie ended and the eleven o'clock news came on. Mrs. Jensen got up and switched off the set. They never had anything but riots and killings and plane crashes on the news. Mrs. Jensen figured there was enough violence and unhappiness in a person's everyday life without watching film of it every night on the news before you went to bed. She went back to the little bathroom off her room and began brushing out her hair.

At eleven-thirty, wearing a clean flannel night-gown and with her hair in rollers, she climbed into bed. Sometimes she watched Johnny Carson for an hour or so until she got sleepy, but tonight she was too tired.

Mrs. Jensen closed her eyes and lay warm and cozy under the down comforter she'd brought with her when she came to work for Mr. Richter. Finding this job after her husband died had been a blessing. She had no other family, and really needed someone to take care of. The house here and Joey were enough to keep her busy, but not more than she could comfortably handle.

She had assumed a sort of housemother position for the man and the boy, which worked out well for all three. When Mr. Richter married his new wife he hastened to assure Mrs. Jensen that her place in the household was secure. Nevertheless, Mrs. Jensen at first had misgivings about the new Mrs. Richter. The slim, pretty blonde from California had seemed too young and unsettled for Mr. Richter. Also, having no children of her own, how was she going to get along with Joey?

As it happened, everything worked out fine. The new Mrs. Richter had turned out to be a lot more mature and sensible than she looked, and she and the boy had taken to each other instantly. And if Mrs. Richter was a tiny touch nervous sometimes, well, that only made Mrs. Jensen feel more useful.

She rolled over onto her back and cleared her mind of all daytime thoughts in preparation for going to sleep.

A shadow passed her window.

Mrs. Jensen sat up in bed and stared at the drawn blind.

Nothing.

And yet there had been something. Just outside. She held her breath and listened.

Nothing.

But something had been there, all right. Olivia Jensen was not the kind of woman who imagined shadows in the night. She got up and pulled on her robe, tying the belt securely beneath her bosom. She went to the window and pulled aside the blind. An expanse of lawn, revealing rose bushes and the back of the garage, brightened occasionally as the clouds broke up and the moon came through. But nothing moved.

Leaving her room, Mrs. Jensen went out and began testing the door and windows of the house, even though she was sure she had locked them all before going to bed. When she reached the living room she heard something.

A rustling sound in the shrubbery outside the front door. She looked through the peep-viewer, but could see nothing. She started to back away, then stopped as she heard a kind of snuffling outside. Then a soft scraping sound as of some animal pawing at the door.

Animal? A dog, she thought. Could her sister's German shepherd have gotten lost and somehow found its way here? It was a long way to where her sister lived, but you read about those things all the time. Maybe it was hurt. Mrs. Jensen opened the door.

The wolf sprang into the air and hit her full in the chest, knocking her to the floor as it tumbled past her into the hallway.

There was no time for Mrs. Jensen to think about what was happening. She could only react by instinct.

The wolf, larger and stronger than any she had seen in the zoo, stood in the hallway, its powerful legs braced. The broad tan head swung to and fro, as though it were looking for something.

Mrs. Jensen stumbled to her feet. The front door was still open, letting the cold air in. Outside, the night was peaceful and clear; inside was terror.

"Get out of here!" she said to the animal. Her voice sounded small and ineffectual.

The wolf swung its head to look at her. The lips slid back to uncover long killer teeth in a devil's grin. It growled deep in its chest, a menacing growl that warned her away.

"Is somebody down there?" Joey's excited treble came clearly from the top of the stairs.

The wolf turned from Mrs. Jensen and looked toward the stairs. With a soft growl it started to move that way.

Acting on the unreasoning instinct to protect the boy, Mrs. Jensen seized the nearest thing at hand that could be used as a weapon—an umbrella from the wooden stand near the door. Brandishing the umbrella like a club, she thrust herself between the wolf and the stairway.

"Joey, get back!" she shouted. "Get in your room and lock the door."

Upstairs the door to the boy's room slammed.

The wolf threw her a look of pure animal hatred and lunged to one side of her, trying to get to the stairs. As the animal went past, Mrs. Jensen struck at it with the umbrella, hitting it across the back. The wolf hesitated. Mrs. Jensen threw herself upon it, clubbing at its head.

The impact of her body knocked the wolf off-balance, and they crashed against the end post of the banister. The wolf was back on its feet immediately, teeth bared, snarling.

Mrs. Jensen scrambled away on the floor, holding the umbrella out toward the wolf like a sword. She heard her own voice screaming incoherent things.

The last thing she saw was the open-mouthed leap of the wolf. She went down helplessly under its weight as the beast brushed aside the puny umbrella. The head turned sideways and the cruel teeth clamped onto her throat. One flex of the powerful jaws crushed the thyroid cartilage and destroyed the larynx and esophagus. The teeth ripped through the platysma muscle and severed the carotid artery. Mrs. Jensen's life ended in a burbling gasp.

The wolf raised its bloody muzzle from the ruined throat and backed away from the body. It turned and started toward the stairs.

13

ONE POWERFUL BOUND carried the wolf a quarter of the way up the stairs. There he stopped suddenly and listened. Outside there was a growing clamor of voices, as the neighbors, roused by Mrs. Jensen's screams, ran toward the Richter house to investigate.

Torn by conflicting emotions, part human, mostly animal, the wolf hesitated. The still-bloody muzzle pointed down toward the open front door, then up the stairs. On the landing, the door to the boy's room was closed. Behind it, the child was crying. The thin wood panel would not keep the huge wolf out for long, but out in front of the house, running feet were already pounding across the lawn.

The wolf chose survival. Leaping gracefully from

the stairs, the beast landed on the floor of the hallway just as the first of the neighbors reached the front door. Without pausing, the wolf raced through the living room and sprang into the air, crashing out through a large window at the side of the house. As a babble of voices came from the house, the wolf loped across the lawn, through a border of trimmed shrubbery, and into the trees beyond.

Down the block, unnoticed by the people swarming toward the Richter house, a white Ford started its engine and moved slowly away from the curb without lights.

Inside, the house all was blood and confusion. The first people to come through the door stopped short at the sight of Mrs. Jensen's torn body. They were jostled forward by those who rushed in after them, and sent skidding off balance on the slippery floor.

A man turned away to vomit.

A woman screamed.

"He went out the window!" someone shouted.

"Let's go after him!"

"No, wait, maybe he's got a gun."

"Somebody call the police."

A woman standing on the fringe of the milling group turned to the man next to her. "It didn't look like a man to me," she said. "It looked like a big dog."

The man only glanced at her, shook his head irritably, and pushed forward for a closer look.

On the landing above them the door to Joey's room opened. The boy came out slowly and walked stiff-legged to the head of the stairs. His face was white and puffy, his eyes wide. One of the men stepped gingerly around Mrs. Jensen's body and ran up the stairs. He picked the boy up in his arms and carried him back into the bedroom.

At one o'clock Karyn and David arrived home to find their street clogged with emergency vehicles, and people swarming over the lawn in front of their house. The mobile-news crew from a local television station had parked its van in the driveway and had set up floodlights illuminating the house and yard. Overhead a police helicopter thundered in a tight circle, sweeping the area with a powerful spotlight.

David jammed to a stop at a wooden police barricade and jumped out of the car. He ran toward the house with Karyn following close behind. A rumpled man with weary eyes headed them off before they reached the front door.

"Just a minute, sir."

"This is our house," David said. "We live here. Who are you?"

"I'm Lieutenant MacCready of the Seattle Police. Are you Mr. and Mrs. Richter?"

"Yes. What's happened?"

"I'm afraid there's been an accident. A serious accident."

"Oh, my God, Joey!" Karyn cried. "Something's happened to Joey!"

"If that's the little boy, ma'am, he's all right," said MacCready. "One of the neighbors took him to their house."

"What is it, then?" David demanded.

"There was an older woman living here—"

"Mrs. Jensen," David said. "She's our house-keeper."

"She's dead, sir. She's been killed."

Karyn's knees turned rubbery for a moment. David put an arm around her shoulder to steady her.

"How did it happen?" he asked the policeman.

"If you could come inside and answer a few questions, you can help us find that out," Mac-Cready said.

David looked down at Karyn.

"It's all right," she said in a small voice.

He turned back to MacCready. "We'll help in any way we can, Lieutenant."

Inside, Mrs. Jensen's body had been taken away and a tarpaulin spread on the floor at the foot of the stairs to cover most of the spilled blood. Lieutenant McCready led the Richters into the family room, out of sight of the blood stains.

Yes, they told him, everything had seemed quite normal when they left the house this evening. No, they had no knowledge of anyone who might want to kill Mrs. Jensen. Yes, she was a careful person, in the habit of keeping the door locked. No, it was not likely she would have admitted a stranger to the house.

Lieutenant MacCready scribbled notes in a spiral-bound pad as Karyn and David answered his questions.

"Have you noticed anyone suspicious hanging around the neighborhood lately?"

Karyn started to speak, then hesitated.

The detective looked up. "Mrs. Richter?"

Karyn saw David's slight frown, but went ahead anyway. "Well, there has been someone. But I don't know if it's relevant."

"Anything at all you can tell me might help," MacCready said.

"There's a woman," Karyn said, getting the words out in a hurry. "I've seen her several times lately. I had the feeling she was following me."

MacCready's eyes narrowed. "A woman following you, you say."

Karyn chewed her lip. She looked over at David. He took her hand.

"Do we have to go through all of this now?" David said to the policeman. "My wife has been under the care of a doctor. For her nerves."

Karyn stiffened slightly at David's emphasis on *nerves.*

"I'll make it as brief as I can," MacCready said. "This could be very important if what we have here is an attempted kidnapping."

"Kidnapping?" Karyn said. "Do you mean someone was trying to take Joey?"

"It's a possibility. Now, about this woman—"

Karyn told him about the dark-haired woman, and how she'd seen her in the coffee shop, on the street, and again riding in the taxi. As she spoke, Karyn realized how thin it sounded, how little it really was to base a suspicion on.

"Are you sure it was the same woman each time?" MacCready asked, his tone cool and courteous.

"Yes. I'm almost certain it was the same woman."

"Almost," the liteutenant repeated under his breath. Karyn could see the interest fade in his eyes. "We'll check it out," he said. "I think that's enough for tonight." He took a card from his breast pocket and handed it to David. "If anything comes up, give me a call."

As MacCready closed his notebook and stood up to leave, another uniformed officer came into the room.

"Lieutenant, do you want to talk to that woman now? The one who says she saw an animal?"

Karyn looked up sharply.

"No," MacCready said shortly. "You take her statement, that's all we need."

"What's that about an animal?" Karyn asked.

David gave her a warning look.

"One of your neighbors said she thought it looked like a big dog that jumped through the window and ran away from the house when the people came in." MacCready dismissed the idea with a wave of his hand. "People sometimes see things like that in moments of stress."

"But is it possible," Karyn persisted, "that it *was* an animal?"

The detective shook his head. "There are no dogs anywhere around here as big as the one she says she saw. And besides—" His eyes flicked toward the archway beyond which lay the blood-spattered tarpaulin. "There's no dog I ever heard of would do that to a human being."

"What about a wolf?" The question was out before she could think about it.

"Karyn, please," David said.

Lieutenant MacCready answered her question seriously. "No way. Wolves need wilderness. The only wilderness around here is that patch of trees over beyond your house, and nothing bigger than a ground squirrel can exist in there. No, what we're looking for here is a man. A big, powerful man. Probably a psychopath."

"I hope you get him, Lieutenant," David said fervently. "Mrs. Jensen was like part of the family."

"Don't you worry, Mr. Richter," said the detective, "we'll get him."

Karyn turned away from the men. Through the window she could see the moon shining intermittently through the broken clouds. *No, you won't, Lieutenant,* she thought. *Not this one.*

14

AFTER THE POLICE and the television people and the neighbors and the sightseers left, David picked up his son from the neighbor's house and took Joey and Karyn to spend the night in a hotel. The next day they took Joey to stay with David's sister, who lived across the lake, in Bellevue. Then they went down to the police station and answered more questions for Lieutenant MacCready. Finally, late in the afternoon, they went back to their house.

David strode around briskly, talking in a very businesslike manner. "We'll have to get the window replaced first thing. And new carpeting in the hall. The stairs and the wall will need a thorough cleaning."

"Do we have to settle it all right now?" Karyn said.

"The important thing," said David, "is to get on with our lives. Get Joey back home and everything back to normal as fast as possible."

"No, David," Karyn said softly. "It won't work. Things will never be back to normal. Whatever that is."

"Please, Karyn, I know this is a terrible blow. I feel it too, believe me. But it won't do any good to dwell on it."

"Don't you understand?" she said. "Don't you know what it was that killed Mrs. Jensen? No, it was not a dog, and it was no psychopathic killer, either."

"You don't seriously believe—"

"I do. The wolves of Drago are here. The werewolves. They've come for me."

"You're upset. I'll call Dr. Goetz. He can prescribe something for your nerves."

"Dr. Goetz can't do me any good now. No one can. They've found me, and there will be no rest now. What happened to Mrs. Jensen is my fault."

"That's crazy talk. It was a prowler, more than likely."

Karyn took both his hands in hers. "It was no prowler, darling. I know that, and I think in your heart you know it too. As long as I stay here, there is danger. Not only for me, but for you and Joey, too."

"What are you saying?"

"I have to go away, David."

"No!" he cried.

"I have no choice."

"But—where will you go? How long will you stay?"

"I'll stay until this thing is over, one way or another. And I think it's better if I don't say where I'm going right away."

"I can't agree to that."

"Please, David. I promise you I'll let you know as soon as I can. Meanwhile, the fewer people who know where I'm going, the harder it will be for anyone to follow me."

"I'll go with you," he said. "We'll fight this out together."

Karyn shook her head. "No, darling. Joey will need at least one of his parents with him. He'll need your strength."

"Karyn, I can't let you just—walk out this way."

"I have to," she said. "It would be too dangerous for you and for Joey if I stayed here. If you love me, David, don't try to stop me."

He put his arms around her and pulled her tight against him. "If I love you? My God, Karyn, I love you more than anything in the world."

Karyn let her head rest on her husband's chest. She heard a sound she had never heard before. David Richter was crying.

The next morning Karyn bought a ticket to Los Angeles at the Western Airlines counter in the

Seattle-Tacoma Airport. She did not notice the old woman, bundled up in scarves, who sold paper flowers nearby. The old woman, however, paid close attention to Karyn.

15

WHEN HER FLIGHT was announced, Karyn hurried to the loading gate, trying not to look at all the people saying affectionate goodbyes. She could still see the puzzled and hurt expression in Joey's eyes as she tried to explain that Mom had to go away for a while. She had hugged him very tight and promised to come back soon. It was a promise Karyn hoped she could keep.

She found her seat on the plane and sat looking out at the rain-slick runway as the jet rolled into position for takeoff. She wished she could be sure this was the right thing to do. Running away, she knew, was never a solution, yet if she stayed to fight she would surely lose. If it were only herself she might have tried, but there were Joey and David to think of. Karyn was sure now that the wolf had been after Joey, and that only Mrs. Jensen's courage and the arrival of the neighbors had saved the boy's life. As long as Karyn was there, the people she loved were in danger.

At last the Western Airline jet received clearance from the tower and thundered down the runway and into the air. In a little while the stewardess came down the aisle, passing out plastic sets of earphones. There was no movie on the short flight, but several channels of recorded stereo music were available. Karyn chose a program of light classics and settled back in the seat, hoping the music would push the troubled thoughts out of her mind, at least temporarily.

But it was no use. Every time Karyn closed her eyes she would see the elusive face of the woman with the white-streaked hair. Or Roy Beatty, who was supposed to be dead, watching her from above. Or the impersonal gray tarpaulin spread over the floor where Mrs. Jensen had died.

How had they found her, Karyn wondered, the wolves of Drago? She was certain now that it was vengeance that had brought the horrors from the past so explosively into her present. Vengeance for her part in the destruction of Drago and most of the unnatural creatures that lived there. Most of them. But not all. Roy had survived. Roy and at least one other.

Marcia!

Karyn jerked upright in the seat so suddenly that the earphones were pulled loose from her head. She saw it now—the woman in the coffee shop, and on the street, and in the taxi. Darken that streak in her hair, take away the sunglasses hiding the green eyes, and you have Marcia Lura. But how could that be? Karyn had fired the gun herself, and had seen the impact at close range as the silver bullet penetrated the skull of the black she-wolf. Never mind how. It was Marcia. Marcia and Roy. And they had come for her.

Karyn sat back in the seat once more, her mind racing. It helped, if only a little, to know what she was up against. Maybe now she could make plans. The stay with her parents could be only temporary. If Marcia and Roy had found her in Seattle, they would find her again. She would not risk endangering any more of her loved ones.

On the telephone to her mother and father, she had been evasive about her reasons for wanting to visit them. They had not pressed her for details. Karyn resolved to stay there only until she could decide on a course of action. What it might be, she had no idea now, but she had to come up with something. She could not live the rest of her life in fear.

The plane made a wide turn over the San Bernardino Mountains and began the long descent to Los Angeles International Airport. Karyn smiled to see her parents waiting for her at the Western Airlines passenger gate.

Frank Oliver was tall and straight with fine white hair that was always carefully combed. His wife, Nancy, had a round, pretty face with smile lines etched at the corners of her eyes. She ran forward to hug her daughter as Karyn came through the walkway from the plane. Frank Oliver came behind her, reserved and dignified, but with the love showing in his eyes.

As they walked out to the parking lot where the Olivers had left their Buick, they all acted as though this were just a normal visit of a daughter to her parents. They compared the weather in Seattle and Los Angeles, they discussed the health of David and Joey, they talked about Karyn's flight down.

During the drive to the Olivers' house in Brentwood, all three ran out of small talk at the same time, and an uncomfortable silence enveloped them.

Karyn's mother, sitting in the back seat while her daughter rode up front with Mr. Oliver, leaned forward and placed a hand gently on Karyn's shoulder.

"Are you all right, dear?" she said.

Karyn patted her mother's hand. She tried to keep her voice casual as she answered. "Of course, Mother. I'm fine."

"I mean *really*," Mrs. Oliver persisted.

Karyn started to say something bland and reassuring, but it caught in her throat. She said, "It's nothing too serious. My nerves acting up, the doctor says. I thought it would do me good to get away for a little while."

"Is it the dreams again?" her father asked. He took his eyes off the road briefly to glance over at her.

"Yes," Karyn admitted. "And other things. I'd rather not talk about it, though. Not right now."

"It's all right, dear," her mother said. "We understand. You stay with us as long as you like, and if there's anything at all we can do, you know we're ready to help."

Karyn turned in the seat to smile at her mother. "I know you are." She reached over to touch her father's arm. "You too, Daddy. You've both been wonderful when I needed you. I'm very lucky."

For the rest of the drive, the conversation returned to inconsequential things. They pulled up to the big, comfortable house on Altair Drive, and Karyn was pleased to see it had not changed at all.

She moved into her old room upstairs in the rear of the house. The room brought back mixed memories: There were her carefree high school days with photos of friends tucked into the frame of the mirror, and posters of the Beatles and Joe Namath on the walls; then there was the nightmarish period right after her breakdown. In the shadows of the room lurked reminders of that time when insanity seemed the easy way out.

Karyn set about unpacking the few things she

had brought with her, and concentrated on keeping her thoughts positive.

It was three days before Karyn finally began to relax. At the dinner table her father told a small joke, and Karyn found to her surprise that she was honestly laughing. It was the first time she had laughed naturally in weeks. She realized then just how tightly wound she had been. At last she was sure that coming home had been the right thing. That night she learned she was wrong.

It was the howling. At first, only half-awake, Karyn thought it was the dream again. She sat up in bed and stared at the window—a charcoal-gray square in the blackness of the room. She waited, praying that it had been only the dream. Then she heard it again. The deep-throated, tortured howl of the werewolf. It had no direction, but seemed to come from everywhere. And it was near. They had found her once more.

The werewolf howled no more that night, but Karyn lay tensely awake. By dawn she was exhausted, her nerves frayed.

At breakfast her mother studied her from across the table. Karyn was sharply aware of her pallor and the shadows around her eyes.

"Didn't you sleep well last night?" Mrs. Oliver asked.

"Not really," Karyn said. "A touch of indigestion, I think. I shouldn't have gone back for seconds on your roast."

She got no answering smile from her mother. Mrs. Oliver continued to study her daughter's face.

"I thought that dog might have kept you awake," she said.

"Dog?"

"Somebody must have left him locked out or something. He made quite a racket about two o'clock." Then, casually, "Didn't you hear it?"

Oh, I heard it all right, Karyn thought, only it wasn't any dog. There was no point, though, in getting into that discussion with her mother. She said, "No, I didn't hear anything."

It was clear that Mrs. Oliver was not fully satisfied, but she did not push it. They closed the topic with a couple of remarks about how people should take better care of their pets.

The breakfast was link sausage and moist scrambled eggs. Ordinarily Karyn would have loved it, but this morning she had little appetite. She ate as much as she could, knowing her mother was watching, but finally had to push the plate away. She was spared answering further questions by the ringing of the doorbell.

Mrs. Oliver excused herself to answer it. Karyn followed her out to the living room and was introduced to a neighbor, Mrs. Gipson, a chunky woman whose face was flushed with excitement.

After briefly acknowledging Karyn, the neighbor turned back to Mrs. Oliver. "Did you hear about the awful thing that happened last night? Over at the Stovalls'?"

"No."

"Somebody killed Zora Stovall's horse!"

"I don't believe it! That beautiful palomino?"

"That's not the worst of it. You should see the way it was done. The poor thing's throat and belly was torn right out. There's two policemen over there now. They say they've never seen anything like it. They say it must be some crazy sadist like the one who was cutting up cows out in the valley a few years back."

Mrs. Oliver glanced worriedly at Karyn.

"Have they any idea who did it?" Karyn asked.

"Not really. They say they've got some leads, but the police always say that. It's a terrible mess. They won't let anybody go out near the corral. Poor Zora is all broken up. She loved that horse."

Karyn had heard enough. She left her mother and Mrs. Gipson looking after her, and went up to her room to begin packing. As she had feared, the wolves of Drago had found her again. There was no doubt in her mind who was responsible for the slaughter of the horse. Now she had to run again.

Abruptly, Karyn's icy calm fell to pieces. She sat down heavily on the bed and began to cry. She could not go on running like this every time Marcia Lura and Roy caught up with her. There was no way she could escape them. They seemed to have no trouble finding her, and could probably take her any time they chose.

Karyn got up and looked at herself in the mirror. She dried her eyes and blew her nose lustily into a Kleenex. Stop this, girl, she told herself. It's time to stand and fight. She felt a little better then, but still knew she could not go up against them alone. And it was futile to try to enlist anyone to help her who did not know the horror. In all the world there was just one man who knew, and might help her now. He had once before. Chris Halloran.

16

IN THE MORNING Karyn rummaged through her things and found an old address book with Chris Halloran's phone number. At the time, he was living at a singles' complex in Marina Del Rey called the Surf King. She called the three-year-old number from a phone in her parents' kitchen while Mr. and Mrs. Oliver were in another part of the house.

After a series of clicks a recorded female voice came over the wire: *The number you have called is out of service. Please check your directory to be sure you have the correct number, then dial again.*

Karyn followed the recorded instructions and again reached the disembodied voice. She banged down the receiver in frustration. She should have expected it, of course. In Southern California, where businesses, buildings, and people come and go overnight, it was a lot to expect that a telephone number would get the same party after three years.

There was still the possibility that Chris lived at the same place, but had changed his telephone to an unlisted number. It was, Karyn decided, worth checking out. She could not give up now. She borrowed the car keys from her father and left the house. It was shortly before noon.

The Buick seemed like an excess of automobile to Karyn after the little Datsun she had driven in Seattle, but it rode smoothly, and the power equipment made it easy to handle. She drove down the San Diego Freeway past Culver City to the Marina turnoff.

The Surf King Apartments consisted of four interconnected buildings in cream-colored masonry with harmonizing pastel balconies. Karyn parked in an area marked *Visitors,* and entered the complex through a palm-flanked gateway. She crossed the red adobe central court and passed the Olympic-sized swimming pool where an assortment of young men and women presented their bodies to the sun. They eyed her speculatively from behind their Foster Grants as she walked by. Karyn ignored them and followed a series of arrows past the sauna and the Jacuzzi to the manager's apartment.

She touched the buzzer, and the door was swept

open by a muscular young man with a full black beard, wearing a T-shirt printed with the Coors logo.

"Hi," he said, "I'm Ron."

"Hello—" Karyn began.

"You're really in luck," he said. "I have a vacancy opening up the first of the week. You'll love it. It's a bachelorette, balcony, built-ins, dishwasher, wet bar, sofa makes into a queen-sized bed. Want to take a look?"

"No, thanks," Karyn told him. "I'm not looking for an apartment."

Ron's smile dimmed.

"I'm looking for someone who lives here. At least he used to. His name is Chris Halloran."

The manager frowned. "Halloran? It doesn't sound familiar, but I've got two hundred units here with people moving in and out all the time. I'll check the list of tenants."

He sat down at a desk and pulled out several sheets of paper with names typed on them. Many were crossed off and inked over. Ron traced a finger down the columns of names.

"Nope, sorry. No Halloran."

"He must have moved," Kayrn said. "I know he was living here three years ago."

"A lot of people come and go in three years," the manager said. "I've only been here four months myself."

"Could you look it up for me?" Karyn said. "You must have the records."

"We have 'em, but they're all locked up out in the back."

Karyn switched on one of her best smiles. "I'd really appreciate it if you could check for me. It's awfully important."

Without much enthusiasm the young man left Karyn sitting on the sofa that probably opened into a queen-sized bed, and he disappeared into another room. After several minutes he came back carrying a ledger-sized book.

"You're right," he said, "Christopher Halloran was in 314-C three years ago. Had the place a year, moved out the next April."

Karyn calculated that Chris had given up his apartment here shortly after their split-up in Las Vegas.

"What was the forwarding address?" she said.

Ron scowled down at the ledger. "There isn't any."

"But there has to be." A note of panic crept into Karyn's voice.

"Well, there isn't," Ron insisted. "There's no law that says you have to give one. Listen, if you're so hot to find this guy, why don't you hire a detective?"

Because there's no time, Karyn thought. I need Chris now, today, before something else happens. Before someone else dies.

"Anything wrong?"

Karyn realized she had been staring right through the manager. She shook her head and managed a smile. "No, nothing. Thanks for your trouble." She turned to leave.

"Sure you don't want to just take a look at that bachelorette? We're building tennis courts, and there're parties three nights a week."

Karyn gave him another small shake of her head and walked on out of the Surf King. The dashboard clock in the Buick told her the day was half gone. She felt a terrible urgency to locate Chris before nightfall.

Her next stop was Techtron Engineering, in Inglewood, near the airport. She went inside and spoke to the personnel manager in his small, functional office.

"Chris Halloran left Techtron two years ago," he said.

Karyn felt a sudden emptiness.

"He took a long leave of absence, and when he came back he was never quite the same. Restless, sort of. We were all sorry to see him go. Everyone here liked Chris. In the last few weeks here, though, he couldn't settle down to handle the routine parts of his job. Said he needed more freedom. So he quit."

Afraid of the answer she would get, Karyn asked the question, "Do you know where he went?"

"Oh, yes."

Hope flickered again.

"Chris and another man who worked here at the time, a man named Walter Eckersall, went into partnership and started their own consulting firm. They were a perfect team. Chris supplied the enthusiasm and the creative thinking, and Walt took care of the solid, practical details."

"Are they still in business?"

"Yes, they are. And doing very well, too. We even call them in to do a job for us now and then."

The personnel man wrote down an address in North Hollywood. Karyn thanked him and hurried out to the Buick. It was mid-afternoon. Time was slipping away.

The building on Lankershim Boulevard was a low, cinderblock structure with clean lines and a modest sign on the front identifying it as E & H Engineering Consultants. Karyn scanned the automobiles parked in the diagonal spaces in front of the building, half-hoping to see Chris's bright red Camaro. It was not there. But of course, she told herself, he would have a different car by now.

Inside, the girl at the reception desk, a chesty brunette, smiled up at her.

"I'd like to see Mr. Halloran," Karyn said.

"Mr. Halloran isn't in," the girl said carefully. "Can Mr. Eckersall help you?"

Karyn's spirits sagged again. Finding someone in real life could be so difficult. In the movies all you did was pick up a phone, and there they were. But in the movies there was always a parking place in front of the bank too. "I'll talk to Mr. Eckersall," she said.

Walter Eckersall was a tall, loose jointed man with bushy brown hair. He wore black-rimmed plastic glasses and spoke in a voice of surprising gentleness.

"You had some business with Chris?" he said.

"Not really," Karyn said. "It's more personal."

Eckersall's eyes shifted their focus to a far corner of the room. "Chris is taking a little vacation just now. If you're a friend of his, you'll know how he appreciates his leisure."

"Yes, I know," Karyn said quickly. "Can you tell me where he's gone?"

Eckersall looked uncomfortable. "Uh, I don't know if I can really, uh—"

"I should tell you," Karyn said, "that there is no romance involved here. My personal business with Chris has nothing to do with his private life."

Eckersall gave her a relieved smile. "Sorry. When an attractive lady comes in looking for Chris I sort of assume—well, never mind that. He's down in Mexico now. Staying at a hotel just outside Mazatlán. The Palacia del Mar."

"Thank you," Karyn said. "And don't worry, you haven't gotten Chris in any trouble."

"There's one more thing I'd better mention," Eckersall said. "He's not down there alone."

Karyn hesitated only a moment. "Knowing Chris," she said, "I didn't think he would be."

Heading back to Brentwood in the late afternoon, Karyn silently cursed the traffic on Sunset Boulevard that slowed her progress. Soon it would be dark, and the night, she knew, belonged to the werewolf.

By the time she reached her parents' house the sun had slipped down behind the Santa Monica Mountains. Darkness fell like a curtain. Karyn put the car away in the garage, then stood outside and swung down the counterbalanced door. She started for the house. Halfway along the walk to the front door her heart froze.

A sound.

Something moving in the bushes.

Karyn turned for one terrified look. It was just a dark shape. A shadow moving among shadows. But there was no mistaking what it was.

Karyn fought off the paralysis and ran for the house. *Please, God, let the door be unlocked!* She banged into the solid oak panel, fumbled a split second for the knob, turned it in her slippery hand and half-fell into the house.

Mr. and Mrs. Oliver, startled, rose from their chairs in the living room. Karyn slammed the heavy door shut and cranked the deadbolt lock into place. Outside something thudded softly against the door. Then there was silence.

Her mother came quickly toward her. "Karyn, what's the matter?"

"Is someone out there?" her father said.

Karyn stood with her back braced against the door and struggled to keep her voice at a normal level. "It's all right. Something startled me for a moment."

Mrs. Oliver put her hands gently on her daughter's shoulders. Frank Oliver reached for the doorknob.

"If somebody's bothering you—" he began.

"No, Daddy, don't go out there!!" Karyn cried. Her father looked at her sharply, and she went on in a quieter tone. "Please, Daddy. For me."

Reluctantly he drew his hand back.

"Is the back door locked?" Karyn asked. "And the windows?"

"Karyn," her father said, "if something's happened, I want to know about it."

"Frank." Mrs. Oliver's tone caught his attention. "It won't do any harm to make sure the place is locked up. And it will make Karyn feel better."

Frank Oliver looked from his wife to his daughter. "Well, sure. All right."

"Could we do it now?" Karyn said. "Right away?"

Mr. and Mrs. Oliver exchanged a look, then began checking the windows. Karyn hurried through the house and tried the back door. She was relieved to find it locked. After making sure the kitchen windows were secure, she relaxed a little. She knew her mother and father thought they were humoring a somewhat neurotic daughter, but that was all right. Better than taking a chance with the thing that was out there somewhere in the night. The beast was taunting her, Karyn felt. Letting her know it could kill her at almost any time it chose. Well, maybe it would pass up one opportunity too many.

She drew a deep breath and walked back into the living room to join her parents.

"Everything's locked up tight," Mrs. Oliver said.

"And double-checked," Frank Oliver added.

Karyn hugged her mother, then went over and took hold of her father's hands. "Thank you both," she said, feeling the depth of her love for these people. "You won't have to worry about this after tonight. I'll be leaving tomorrow."

"Leaving?" said her mother. "I'd hoped you could stay longer. A week or so, at least."

"I wish I could," Karyn said, "but there's something I have to settle once and for all before I can ever stay anywhere comfortably again."

She waited. Both of her parents wanted very badly to ask her questions. It showed plainly in their faces. Where was she going? Why? For how long? But, God bless them, they held their questions inside.

"I promise I'll tell you all about it," she said, "when I come back."

I'll tell you *something*, anyway, she thought. Something you can believe.

When I come back.

If I come back.

It was a long and sleepless night, but in the morning she was still alive.

17

A FRESH BREEZE flowed in off the Gulf of California, bringing relief to the damp heat of the Mazatlán summer. North of the city, where the tropical forest pushed close to the shoreline, the Palacio del Mar Hotel occupied a half-moon of beach.

On the stretch of white sand in front of the hotel Chris Halloran lay on a beach blanket. He was propped on his elbows, eyes shaded by a tattered straw hat, as he watched a pretty, auburn-haired girl play in the light surf.

The Palacio was generally favored by an older, quieter clientele than that favoring the new high-rise resorts which had gone up in the city. Chris liked the older hotel because it felt like Mexico.

The pastel stucco of the main beach area was not much different from Miami Beach or Waikiki. At the Palacio you could hear Spanish spoken by the fishermen who came down from the village of Camarón, and you could smell the heady aroma of chiles from the kitchen where the hotel employees ate.

Two of the employees walked by on the path bordering the stretch of beach where Chris lay. Roberto, a handsome lad of seventeen, carried a tray of iced tea for a couple from Indianapolis who sat up the beach protecting their sunburns under one of the hotel's umbrellas. Dancing along at Roberto's side was Blanca, saucy and pert in her maid's uniform, her arms loaded with fresh towels for the cabanas. The eyes of the boy and girl spoke intimately to each other.

Ah, young love, thought Chris Halloran as he watched them pass. Had he ever been in love like that? And once you lost it, could you ever get it back?

At the edge of the water, Audrey Vance stood barely covered by a pink bikini. Her slim, tanned legs were planted apart in the sand. She beckoned for Chris to come and join her.

Chris smiled at her and waved no thanks. Audrey was an actress who photographed like a dream, but couldn't act her way into a high-school play. Thus, her appearances on various television series were mainly decorative. Chris had enjoyed her enthusiasm during their stay in Mazatlán, but he was beginning to think it was time he went back to work.

Audrey struck a pouting pose and shook her head at him in exasperation. Chris tipped the straw hat down over his eyes and lay back on the beach towel.

A moment later, cool droplets of saltwater splashed on his chest and stomach as Audrey stood over him shaking out her hair.

"Come on," she said, "swim with me."

"I'm resting."

"Shit, you can rest any time. I want somebody to swim with me." She reached down and lifted the hat from his eyes. "Maybe I'll go and ask that beautiful young stud who works around here. That Roberto. I'll bet he'd come swimming with me."

"He might at that," Chris said, "but you might have a problem with his girlfriend."

"Come on, Chris, don't be an old fart." She kicked sand across his bare stomach, then ran lightly toward the water, laughing back over her shoulder at him.

With a sigh Chris pushed himself to his feet and jogged over the sand after the girl. While he was in Los Angeles Chris kept in shape with twice-weekly workouts at the gym, along with tennis and handball. Swimming, however, had never appealed to him. Even when he lived at the marina, he rarely used the swimming pool, and went to the beach only to play volleyball.

He followed Audrey as she splashed happily into the surf. The water was bathtub warm, and the waves were low and gentle. The girl swam easily ahead of him with long graceful strokes while he tried to keep up with his own windmilling version of the crawl.

Fifty yards offshore, Audrey stopped and waited for him, treading water. When he splashed up beside her she wrapped her arms and legs around him and gave him a big open-mouthed kiss. They sank together slowly below the surface.

Chris came up sputtering and blowing as the girl bobbed up like a dolphin beside him.

"What are you trying to do, drown me?" he said between coughs.

Audrey tossed the wet hair out of her eyes and laughed at him. Chris tried and failed to hold a stern expression.

"You're crazy, you know that?" he said.

She swam over close to him and slipped one hand under the waist band of his trunks. "Have you ever screwed under water?"

"Sure, lots of times."

Abruptly the girl's mood changed. She backed off and looked at him. "You've done just every damn thing, haven't you?" Without waiting for a response, she struck out toward the beach.

No, he thought as he swam slowly after her, not quite everything. Sometimes, though, it seemed he was trying. Until three years ago he had lived a fairly quiet bachelor life. He raised a little hell on weekends, did his share of womanizing, but on the whole led a life devoid of extreme highs and lows. Then came the urgent call for help from Karyn Beatty. Answering that call had plunged Chris into a night of hell in the mountain village of Drago, and had changed his life forever.

After the horror of Drago and the fire that destroyed it, there had been the nerve-shattering six months he and Karyn had spent trying to run away from it. When he finally returned to reality he had quit his job and gone into partnership with solid Walt Eckersall, who allowed him to take off two or three months a year. He had moved out of the swinging-singles apartment and rented a house in Benedict Canyon, where he could party when he felt like it and be left alone when he wanted to. When he worked he worked hard, and when he played he went to places like the Kona Coast or Curaçao or Mazatlán. Sometimes he went with a woman, sometimes by himself.

Chris knew that his life-style was designed to help him forget the past. Most of the time it worked, but for some reason he had lately found himself often thinking of Karyn. He had never shaken the nagging guilt he felt for not going to see her at her parents' home after the Las Vegas crack-up.

What the hell, he told himself for the hundredth time. She got better, didn't she? After the way things ended, seeing him would have done nothing to help her condition. It could easily have made things worse. Chris put his head down in the water and stroked powerfully toward the shore.

Audrey was waiting for him when he waded up onto the beach. Her momentary irritation was all over.

"About Goddamn time, slowpoke. I thought I was going to have to swim out and haul you in."

"Why do you think I was stalling?" he said.

"I thought maybe you were daydreaming about some old girlfriend."

Chris looked at her quickly, but saw she was just kidding. One of those unconscious intuitive flashes women seemed to get. If they ever harnessed that power, he thought, they could rule the world.

He said, "Do you want to go get some lunch?"

Audrey lowered her eyes demurely and peeked up at him through thick, moist lashes. "Do I have another choice?"

"My God, woman, you're insatiable."

"Damn right, big fella, and you love it. Come on, I'll help you shower off the salt."

They walked hand in hand up from the beach and along the wide veranda of the old Spanish-style building that was the original hotel. In the early 1960s, six separate cabanas had been built on either side of the main building, following the curve of the beach. Chris and Audrey turned in at Number 7, the nearest to the main building, on the south side.

An hour and a half later Chris lay face down, naked, on the bed. His face was pressed against the pillow, his body completely relaxed. Audrey moved restlessly around the room, her tanned body glowing in the light from the afternoon sun that filtered between the slats of the bamboo shades.

"Why do men always want to go to sleep afterwards?" she said.

"Mmmpff," Chris muttered into the pillow.

"It always pumps me full of energy. Makes me want to get moving and do things."

Chris rolled over onto his side and looked at her. "We already did things."

She dropped into one of the two rattan chairs and stroked herself between the legs. "Good things." She gave him a mischievous look. "I'll bet I could get you interested again."

He sat up and swung his feet off the bed. "No question about it, but first let's go get some lunch."

"Okay, spoilsport."

"Got to keep up my strength, honey. A man my age needs a balanced diet."

"A man your age," she mocked. "Jesus, thirty-three is really getting up there, isn't it?"

"Hand me my pants," he said.

Audrey took a pair of white jeans from the back

of the chair where she was sitting and carried them to the bed. As she handed them to Chris, something fell out of the pocket and hit the grass carpet with a tiny thump. Audrey dropped to her knees and looked around on the floor for a moment. Then she reached under the bed and came out with a small silver object. She held it out to Chris in the palm of her hand.

"What's this?" she said. "I've never seen it before."

Chris's expression sobered. "It's nothing." He held out his hand. "Here, I'll take it."

"It looks like a bullet."

The tiny lump of metal winked up at Chris. It was a bullet, all right. A twenty-two caliber long rifle bullet of pure silver. There had been twelve of them, made to Chris's order by a bemused Los Angeles gunsmith. On the night of the werewolves in Drago, he had fired eleven of them. Karyn had fired the last. Chris had returned just once to the burned-out village, and the bullet had gleamed up at him like an eye from the blackened earth. He had pocketed the bullet and never gone near the place again.

"It's just a toy," he said to Audrey. "Let's have it."

"Another secret," Audrey said, sulking. "You never tell me anything really important about yourself."

"What do you mean, honey? I'm an open book."

"No, I'm serious. I know that little bullet has some important meaning for you. Why won't you share it with me?"

"Because it's none of your business."

Audrey closed her fist around the bullet and marched across the room to the closet, where she began rattling coat hangers irritably. "I'll bet it was a present from that woman."

"What woman?"

"*The* woman. The one you had the hot rocks for and was married to your best friend."

Chris studied the bare back of the girl as she sorted through the clothes hanging in the closet. Either she was a lot more perceptive than he gave her credit for, or he was talking in his sleep.

"Get dressed," he said. "I'm hungry."

As they sat in the hotel dining room awaiting their lunch, the conversation was strained and artificial. It was as though a third person sat unseen at their table, listening.

18

THE AIRPORT AT Mazatlán was small by United States standards. Karyn Richter unbuckled her seat belt as the Aeronaves 727 rolled to a stop. From the window by her seat she watched with amazement the number and variety of aircraft landing, taking off, taxiing, waiting, and just sitting there. There were sleek new jets, old DC-3s, corporate Lears, private Cessnas and Pipers, and even a battered old open-cockpit biplane. Karyn could see no pattern to their movements, but she assured herself that somewhere a control tower was directing the traffic. Nevertheless, compared to big, orderly LAX, it was like a downtown intersection on Christmas Eve.

When the door was opened she joined the other

146

passengers and filed out and down the stairway that had been rolled up to the plane. She crossed the expanse of black tarmac to the terminal building.

Inside it was hot and crowded. Over the noise of arriving and departing passengers announcements rattled continually over the PA system loudspeakers, first in Spanish, then English. Karyn located the baggage-claim counter and after an hour was finally reunited with her bag. She carried it out of the terminal building and set it down on the sidewalk. The air outside was fresh and cool with a hint of the sea, and she inhaled gratefully.

"Carry your suitcase, lady?"

The voice close behind her startled Karyn. She turned to see a tall, pockmarked youth grinning at her through bad teeth. The end of a wooden match protruded from one corner of his mouth.

"No, thank you," she said, and turned away.

"Ah, come on, lady, you don' wan' to carry that heavy thin' all by yourself."

Karyn looked pointedly up the street, trying to ignore him.

"I'm real strong. I can carry anythin' you got. Wan' to see my muscle?"

"I don't need anything carried." She tried to keep the apprehension from showing in her voice.

The youth picked up her bag and backed off, hefting it. "See? It's not too heavy for me."

"Please," Karyn said, trying to sound authoritative, "put that down. It belongs to me."

"Ah, lady, you don' wan' to talk like that."

"*Ay, chico!*" A deep male voice snapped off the words like a whip. The startled boy looked over Karyn's shoulder, and she turned too to see who had spoken.

A square-bodied man with an enormous Zapata moustache glared at the boy. He spoke in hard-edged street Spanish, punctuating his words by jabbing a finger down at the sidewalk.

The boy's insolent grin fell away. He set the bag down at Karyn's feet and started to back off.

The stranger spoke again in Spanish. His voice was soft, but the words were unmistakably a command.

The boy's eyes shifted over to Karyn. "I'm sorry, lady," he muttered, then slipped away into the crowd coming out of the building.

"Permit me to offer apology for my city, señora," said the man with the moustache. "That boy was a *rufían*, a bad one. We are not all like him. There are many good people in Mazatlán."

"I'm sure there are," Karyn said. "Thank you."

The man gestured toward a mud-spattered, ten-year-old Plymouth parked at the curb. The white painted letters *TAXI* were barely visible on the door under a coating of dirt. "The taxi of Luis Zarate is at your service, señora. Also guide service, if you desire."

"Well—I could use a taxi," Karyn said. "Can you take me to the Palacio del Mar Hotel?"

"Con mucho gusto, señora," said Luis Zarate. With a flourish he swept open the rear door of the Plymouth and gestured Karyn inside. He carried her bag to the rear and put it in the trunk, which he closed by tying the lid to the bumper with a frayed length of electric cord.

"The Palacio is a beautiful hotel," he said when he was in position behind the wheel. "It is old and comfortable, and not so big that they forget about you."

"That's nice," Karyn said, without really listening.

Luis started the car and they pulled away from the curb with a grinding of gears and the roar of an unmuffled engine. As he drove, Luis proudly pointed out the sights of the city—the twin golden spires of the cathedral, the old Farol lighthouse looming off-shore, the busy fishing docks—until he sensed that Karyn was not paying attention.

"The señora is troubled?" he said.

Karyn looked up sharply. "What's that?"

Luis Zarate's dark, liquid eyes regarded her seriously from the rear-view mirror. "Forgive me, señora, I do not mean to speak out of my place. But I am a gypsy, *comprende,* and through my blood I have a gift for knowing when someone is in trouble."

"Really?" Karyn said. "You're a gypsy?"

Luis' eyes twinkled at her. "Well, a little bit. My great-grandmother on my mother's side was said to be a gypsy. Anyway, it talkes only a little such blood to make you a gypsy, no?"

"I suppose so," Karyn said, smiling.

They drove on in silence for a mile before the taxi driver spoke again. "The señora is visiting Mazatlán all alone?"

Karyn answered carefully. "No, I—I'm meeting a friend at the hotel."

"It is well. Mazatlán is a beautiful city, and visitors are welcome, but as you have seen, there are bad people here as there are in all cities. It is not wise for a lady to travel too much alone." He was silent for a moment, then added, "You will be here long?"

"I don't know," Karyn said. "Not very."

"Forgive me," said Luis with a little shrug. "I ask too many questions. I jus' thought maybe the señora could use a guide. Someone who will charge you a fair price, and who knows Mazatlán and the jungles and hills behind the city like the lines in his own hand."

Karyn could not suppress a smile. "Someone like Luis Zarate?"

"Sí, señora. Forgive my boast, but it is the truth."

"I appreciate the offer," Karyn said, "but I don't think I'll be doing much sightseeing."

"Eh, *bien,* you will keep Luis Zarate in mind, yes?"

"Yes," Karyn told him, "I will."

Luis drove on out of the city and along a stretch where tree branches with broad green leaves overhung the road on both sides. They turned back toward the sea then and followed the lip of a bluff for a short distance before starting down to the crescent of beach belonging to the Palacio del Mar. Karyn was pleased by the symmetry of the white main building with its red-tiled roof and the cabanas, like miniature copies, extending in a curved row on either side like arms embracing the beach.

As Luis drove along the roadway skirting the beach Karyn looked for Chris Halloran, but did not see him. The closer she came, the more her nerves jumped. There were so many questions. What would be his reaction to seeing her? Would he reject her? Was it fair for her to come back into his life bringing a horror that was no longer his concern? For a moment Karyn had a wild impulse to order the taxi around and head back to the airport. But then where would she go? There was no place left. There was no one else to go to.

"Señora?"

At the sound of the driver's voice, Karyn realized they had come to a stop before the hotel's wide Spanish-style veranda.

Luis jumped out and opened the door for her with another flourish. He retrieved her bag from

the tied-down trunk and followed as Karyn walked
up the steps and into the tiled lobby of the old
hotel. She crossed to the registration desk, where
a light-complexioned man with a high arched nose
watched her with a small professional smile. A
metal plate on the counter before him spelled out
in raised letters: *J. Davila, Manager.*

"Good afternoon, señora," he said.

Karyn nodded to acknowledge the greeting. "I'm
looking for a gentleman I understand is registered
here. Mr. Halloran."

A shadow flickered across the manager's eyes.
"Ah, yes, Señor Halloran. You are—a relative?"

"No, I'm a friend. If he's registered here, I'd like
to see him, please."

Señor Davila checked his registration cards in
a businesslike manner. He pulled one of the cards
out of the file and examined it. "Yes, Mr. Halloran is one of our guests."

"May I have his room number?"

"He is registered in Cabana Number 7."

"Thank you. Is there a phone I can use to call
him?"

"I am sorry, there are no telephones in the cabanas."

"Then if you'll show me where it is, I'll go and
find him myself."

"Ah, but that would be of no use. Señor Halloran
is not in his cabana now."

Karyn's temper began to fray. "Well, where is

he? I came here to see Mr. Halloran, and I don't have time to waste."

Luis Zarate stepped up to the desk. "Permit me, señora," he said, then spoke briefly in Spanish to the man at the desk. When he had finished, the hotel manager turned to Karyn with an apologetic smile.

"Señnor Halloran is presently at lunch in our dining room," he said.

"Thank you," Karyn said coolly. "Now if you will just tell me where the dining room is—"

Davila looked uncomfortable. "I am obliged to tell the señora that Señor Halloran is not lunching alone."

"Oh, for heaven's sake, so he has a girl with him. It makes no difference to me. What did you think— that I was his wife?"

"One is never sure," said Davila. The relief was evident in his expression. "Permit me to show you to the dining room, señora."

"Do you wish me to wait?" asked Luis.

"No," Karyn said, "I don't think so." She paid the fare and added a generous tip.

"*Muchas gracias,*" said the taxi driver. "You will not forget, if you need any form of assistance while you are in Mazatlán, no one is better prepared to deliver than Luis Zarate."

"I won't forget," Karyn assured him.

Luis deposited her bag behind the registration desk and walked back out the entrance. Davila came around the desk and Karyn followed him out through the lobby and beneath an archway into the dining room.

It was a big bright room with sunlight streaming in through tall windows along one wall. The tables were widely spaced, covered with clean white linen and set with gleaming silver.

It took Karyn only a moment to find Chris. He hadn't changed much, she thought. Still the same firm features, the unruly brown hair, and as always a deep tan. He was a touch more serious around the eyes, maybe. But who wouldn't be, after two years?

Chris was seated facing Karyn, but not looking in her direction. On the near side of the table sat a girl with long, shiny auburn hair. From the way the girl sat erect and held her head cocked to one side, Karyn could tell she was young and lively. Karyn was surprised at the pang of jealousy.

The hotel manager started to lead the way across the room to Chris's table.

"Never mind," Karyn said. "I see him."

She walked alone toward the table. When she was ten feet away Chris looked up and saw her. Ever since she had left Los Angeles, Karyn had tried to prepare for this moment when she and Chris Halloran faced each other again after two years apart. However, she was not ready for the montage of memories, good and bad, that flashed across her mind. Chris's face reflected many of the same emotions she felt, with the added shock of seeing her so unexpectedly. He sat frozen for a moment, then rose from his chair.

"Karyn. What—what a surprise."

"Hello, Chris."

"It's been a while."

"Yes. It has."

They stood for a moment looking at each other, with a thousand things to say, and nothing that could be said.

The girl sitting at the table set her water glass down with a distinct thump. Chris looked down suddenly, as though surprised at finding her there.

"I'm sorry," he said. "Karyn, this is Audrey Vance. Audrey, an old friend of mine, Karyn Beatty."

"It's Karyn Richter now."

"Oh. I see. Excuse me."

Audrey looked up from her chair with a dazzling smile. She ran her eyes over Karyn appraisingly. "It's a pleasure to meet you, Mrs. Richter. I haven't met many of Chris's old friends."

Karyn wondered if she detected a faint emphasis on *old*. "Please call me Karyn," she said.

Chris glanced warily from one woman to the other. "Have you had lunch, Karyn?" he said quickly. "Won't you join us?"

"Yes, please do," said Audrey.

"I ate on the plane," Karyn said, "but I could use a cup of coffee."

Chris pulled out a chair for her and signaled the waiter.

"I don't think you'll like the coffee in Mexico, Karyn," Audrey said. "It always tastes like they left it brewing overnight. Chris and I usually have the tea."

"That's all right," Karyn said, returning the younger woman's smile. "I like my coffee strong."

The waiter brought a muddy black brew in a heavy mug. Karyn sipped at it and made a show of enjoying the taste.

For the next few minutes Chris made an awkward attempt at small talk while Karyn responded politely and noncommittally. Audrey ate in silence, alert for any vibrations between Chris and Karyn.

Finally Chris ran out of inconsequential remarks. He said, "I, uh, don't suppose you're down here by sheer coincidence."

"No," Karyn said. "I came looking for you."

"Well, you found me."

"It couldn't have been easy," Audrey put in.

"It wasn't," Karyn admitted.

An edgy minute of silence dragged by.

"Are you staying here at the hotel?" Audrey asked finally, holding her smile in place.

"I'm not sure yet," Karyn said. Abruptly she turned to Chris. "I have to talk to you."

"I suppose that means *alone*," Audrey said, her smile gone brittle.

"If you don't mind too much," Karyn said. "I'm sure you can spare him for a few minutes."

"Oh, I suppose I can." Audrey stood up and stretched her lithe young body. She walked behind Chris's chair and traced a forefinger along the back of his neck. "I'll be in our room, darling."

Chris's eyes followed her as she walked out.

"Pretty girl," Karyn said when they were alone.

"Yes," Chris said, dismissing the subject. "What's happened?"

Karyn looked around the dining room. The orderliness of the place and the well-dressed, well-mannered guests enjoying lunch seemed inappropriate for what she had to tell.

"Can we go somewhere else?"

"Sure." Chris signed the check and they walked out of the hotel and down across the beach. They passed the somnolent sunbathers and continued to the wet, packed sand at the water's edge. They walked on to where the sandy beach ended and there were rocks in the surf, and the jungle grew right down to the sea. They sat down on a big rock and watched the incoming waves churn into a green and white froth.

"Do you remember the fire at Drago?" Karyn said, looking out to sea.

"Could I ever forget it?"

"And afterward, how we heard the howling and knew that not all the wolves had died?"

"We don't know that for sure, Karyn. What we

heard might have been coyotes or something, and not those—creatures from Drago."

Karyn shook her head. "No, it was the were-wolves. I know, because they've come for me."

As calmly as she could, Karyn told him about the things that had happened since she first had the feeling of being watched, less than a month ago in Seattle. She told of seeing Roy in the shopping mall, of the death of Mrs. Jensen, of the flight to her parents' home in Los Angeles and the signs that the wolves had followed her there, too.

Chris sat for a long moment when she had finished her story. Finally he said, "And you think one of them who's come for you is Roy?"

"I'm sure of it. I saw him."

"You couldn't be mistaken?"

"No. And that woman, Marcia Lura, is one of them too."

"Are there any more?"

"I don't know. I don't think so. Just the two of them."

There was another heavy pause before Chris spoke again. "All right, what do you want me to do?"

Karyn turned away suddenly, trying not to cry. "I—I don't know, Chris. I came here because I didn't have anyone else. I can't fight them alone."

Her control crumbled then and she began to sob. Tears spilled freely down her cheeks. Chris put an arm around her and eased her head down on his shoulder.

The words came tumbling out between sobs. "This isn't fair to you, Chris. This isn't your fight. You don't owe me anything. I ran away from my husband and our little boy because I was afraid that if I stayed they'd be hurt. Now I've come here and probably put you in danger. I'm so sorry. I just didn't know what else to do." She made an effort to pull free. "I'll leave now, before anyone gets hurt. I'll go back to—I'll go somewhere. I should never have come."

Chris pulled her head back against him. "Cut it out. Of course you had to come to me. There's nobody else who knows these creatures exist, who has seen what they can do. Now settle down, and we'll think of something."

Karyn relaxed and let herself lean against him. Slowly her sobs quieted. She sat up and borrowed his handkerchief to dry her eyes.

"Is there anything we can do, Chris? Can we really fight them?"

"We fought them before," he said. "We just didn't finish the job. Do you think they've followed you here yet?"

"I haven't seen any signs, but they seem to know my movements."

"Well, let's assume we have a little time, anyway. We'll get you checked into the hotel now, and tomorrow we'll start making plans."

They stood up together, and for a moment each looked deeply into the other's eyes. Chris's arms went around her, and Karyn without thinking pressed her body against him. He kissed her long and deeply, and she could feel him becoming aroused.

It was Chris who stepped back first. He said, "Let's go see about getting you a room."

They walked back across the beach to the hotel without speaking.

Señor Davila, the manager, was all gracious attention now. "Ah, señora, you are in luck. This is our busy time of the year, but we do have one late cancellation. Cabana Number 12. I can put you in there."

"Which one is that?" Karen asked.

"It is at the far end of the row where Señor Halloran has his."

"You have nothing here in the main building?"

"I am sorry, señora."

"That's all right. I'll take it."

Chris squeezed her arm. "I'd better go and square things with Audrey. I think she's a little ticked off at being left alone. We'll see you at dinner."

Karyn completed her registration, and a handsome boy of about seventeen, who introduced himself as Roberto, carried her bag along the path to her cabana. Inside it was not lavish, but it was clean. There was a double bed, bureau, night table, and two chairs and a settee of wicker. Roberto showed her the small closet and the bathroom, and demonstrated how to open the window and operate the heater. Karyn tipped the boy and promised to ask for him personally if there was anything she needed.

As Roberto went out, a young maid with sparkling eyes and lush, moist lips came in with fresh towels. A look flashed between the two young people that told Karyn they were much more than friends.

When the girl left Karyn kicked off her shoes and stretched out on the bed. She closed her eyes and let her mind drift, steering it away, for now, from the dark things she wanted to avoid. An hour later she sat up feeling refreshed and thinking maybe everything would be all right.

She soaked in a hot tub, then took a cool shower and dressed in a light blue knit outfit, which, she knew, showed off her figure. When Chris and Audrey came to take her to dinner, the look in the girl's eyes told Karyn she had chosen well.

During the meal Karyn's feeling of well-being slipped away. The conversation was perfunctory and strained. She could tell there had been an argument between Chris and Audrey, and it made her uncomfortable. As soon as she could, Karyn excused herself, saying she was tired and wanted to go to bed early.

Back in her room Karyn checked the locks on the windows and the door. She turned on all the lights, but the bulbs were of low wattage and did not drive the shadows out of the corners. The cabana cooled off quickly once the sun was down, and Karyn turned up the heater while she got ready for bed.

The sheets were clean and starchy, the pillows thinner than she liked. Karyn lay for a long time in the dark, listening to the whisper of the surf and the night cries from the jungle. She drifted at last into an uneasy sleep.

The late flight south from Los Angeles banked into a gentle turn and began its descent to scattered lights of Mazatlán, nestled between the black jungle and the black ocean. Back in the tourist section, a broad-shouldered man with pale hair dozed fitfully in his too-narrow seat. Beside him at the window a woman gazed down at the expanding lights of the city. Her eyes smoldered with deep green fires. Unconsciously she touched the streak of white that ran through her midnight hair.

19

WHEN THE MORNING came the sun was bright and hot. The ocean was a calm, bottle-glass green, and the fears of the night were not so terrifying. Karen was hungry when she awoke. Her first thought was to find Chris and have him join her for breakfast. Then she remembered that Chris was not alone. Best she stay out of his way for now. In her brief sizing up of Audrey Vance, Karyn had caught the clear message: "He's mine." There were surely enough problems without causing any more friction there. Karyn could wait until there was a chance to see Chris alone to talk about their plans.

There was a discreet knock at the door. Karyn pulled on a robe over her pajamas and went to see who it was. Outside the door stood Roberto.

He held a tray with a pot of steaming coffee, a cup, and a sweet roll. Behind him, on the walk that led past the cabanas, Karyn saw a metal cart with more trays and coffee pots.

"*Buenas días,* señor. Your morning coffee, compliments of the hotel."

"Thank you." Karyn smiled at the boy's obvious pride in his little speech.

"Do you wish sugar? Milk?"

"No, thank you. I drink it black."

"If there is anything more you wish, señora, please call for me."

"All right, Roberto, I'll remember. *Muchas gracias.*"

The boy's smile widened at her use of the Spanish phrase. "*De nada,* señora."

The boy went away, and Karyn took the coffee inside. She poured herself a cup and sipped at it. The brew was murky and strong, but better than no coffee at all.

She showered and dressed and strolled down the walk past the other cabanas toward the main building. She noticed the blinds were drawn in Number 7. She continued into the main building, through the lobby and into the dining room where several other guests were having breakfast.

Karyn chose a table apart from the others and looked over the menu. She passed up huevos rancheros and anything else that sounded Mexican, and ordered straight-up fried eggs. The eggs were not bad, but the toast was dry and the potatoes were fried to crisp brown cubes. The coffee was no better than usual, but Karyn was determined to drink it every chance she got, just to spite Audrey Vance.

After breakfast she went back to her cabana and put on a pair of shorts and a light blouse. She had not thought to pack a swimming suit, considering the nature of her business here. She walked out onto the beach, and young Roberto came running up to provide her with a folding chair down by the tideline.

Karyn adjusted the chair so she could see the row of cabanas and the front of the hotel. Shortly before noon Chris came out, blinking at the sunlight. He started for the surf, then saw Karyn and veered over toward her. He wore brief white swim trunks, and Karyn could not help noticing the smooth tan on his well-muscled body.

"Good morning," he said.

"Hi. I hope you didn't interrupt anything important just to come out and talk to me."

"Don't you start now. I'm getting enough static from Audrey. She thinks the only reason you came down here was for my body."

"Oh? What did you tell her?"

"Nothing. It's easier to let her believe that than to try to explain the real reason."

"I see what you mean."

Both of them were silent for a moment, looking out to sea.

"Did you come up with any ideas?" Karyn said.

Chris sat down on the sand next to her chair. He continued to look out over the water as he spoke. "The way I see it, there isn't much we can do until they make a move."

Karyn whirled on him. "Make a move? You mean until they attack someone else?"

He faced her soberly. "Have you got a better idea?"

"I—oh, I don't know. I guess I expected you to magically solve all my problems. I'm sorry, Chris. I shouldn't have come here. It's not fair to drag you into this again."

"Cut it out," he said. "You came to me because there is no one else. It was the right thing to do. Now settle down and we'll try to approach this logically." After a moment he added, "If it's possible to be logical about werewolves."

Karyn drew a deep breath and gave him a small smile. "All right, let's be logical. Where do we start?"

"Do you expect them to follow you down here?" Chris said. "Marcia and Roy?"

"I'm positive they will. It took them no time at all to find me in Los Angeles. I don't know how, but they seem to know my movements. I wouldn't be surprised if they were here already."

"Okay, let's assume the worst. They're in Mazatlán, and they know where you are. Our best chance is to find them in the daytime. They have no special powers then. Once the sun goes down and they can take on the wolf shape, no man is a match for them. Nothing can stop them in that form except fire and silver."

"So if we don't want to meet them at night, how do we go about finding them in the daylight?"

"We don't," Chris said. "They find us. Find *you,* rather. You're the one they're after. Even with all the power the night gives them, they can't move around freely as wolves without attracting a lot of attention. As you saw up in Seattle, they found you in their human shape first, then when they were ready to attack they came as wolves. It's up to us to be alert, always watching, during the day."

"And at night?" Karyn said.

"At night we are careful as hell."

"Do you think they'll be clumsy enough to let us see them in the daytime?"

"I don't think clumsy has anything to do with it," Chris said. "I think letting you see them was all part of their plan. It was meant to frighten you before they attacked."

"Well, they sure succeeded," Karyn said.

A slim shadow fell across the sand at their feet. "Hey, how cozy."

Karyn looked up and saw Audrey Vance standing behind her chair. The girl smiled tightly and let her eyes flick back and forth between Karyn and Chris. There was no doubt about it, Karyn thought. The girl did have a body. Her pink one-piece swim suit was thin enough and tight enough to emphasize her nipples and the bush of pubic hair.

"Hi," Chris said. "Ready for lunch?"

"Yes, if you haven't already had yours."

Chris ignored the sarcasm. He stood up and brushed the sand from his trunks. "I'll go get wet and be with you in a minute." To Karyn he said, "Damned if the girl isn't making a swimmer out of me."

He loped down to the water and splashed into the surf while the women watched. He dived into an incoming wave and disappeared from sight momentarily, bobbing up again as the wave rolled over him and broke on the shore.

"Have you known Chris a long time?" Audrey asked.

"Yes. He was a friend of my first husband."

"No kidding."

There could not have been, Karyn figured, more than seven or eight years' difference between her own and Audrey's ages, yet Audrey Vance made her feel positively middle-aged. She was acutely aware of her awkward position, sitting in the low folding chair while Audrey stood, straight and slim, a little behind her. Karyn stood up and faced the younger woman and felt better.

"Let's get something straight here," she said. "Whatever you and Chris are to each other makes no difference to me. I wish you both good luck or happiness, or anything else you're after. Chris is a friend of mine, and I'm here to see him as a friend. That's all."

"Sure you are." Audrey made her eyes wide and childlike. "What else could it be?"

Karyn met Audrey's baby stare for a moment, then turned away.

"Shit," she said.

If Audrey heard, she gave no sign.

Chris came jogging back from the surf scrubbing the salt water out of his hair.

"Let's go," he said to Audrey. Then to Karyn: "Want to have lunch with us?"

Karyn hesitated for a moment, just to give the girl something to think about. Then she said, "No, thanks. I had a big breakfast."

Chris and Audrey walked off toward their cabana. Audrey tucked her hand possessively under his arm. Karyn turned back to the beach and saw the young Roberto raking the sand smooth. She beckoned to him and he came running to her, his smile dazzling in the sunlight.

"*Sí*, señora?"

"Could you get me an umbrella, Roberto? I think I've had enough sun for today."

The boy nodded eagerly and took off at a run toward the rear of the hotel. In a few minutes he came back carrying a huge beach umbrella which had alternating panels of orange and green. He planted it in the sand next to Karyn's chair and opened it, taking care to adjust it so she was properly shaded.

Karyn reached into her bag, then looked up apologetically. "I'm afraid I left my money in the room."

"Is no problem, señora," said Roberto. "If you want to give me a tip, is plenty of time when you check out." Still smiling, he trotted off to attend to another guest who was holding up an empty high-ball glass.

Left alone, Karyn settled back with the umbrella shading her from the glare of the sun. She closed her eyes, lulled by the susurration of the surf, and dozed in the gentle breeze. Some time later she awoke with a start. The sun had moved to the west and the shadow of the umbrella had crept up to expose her feet and ankles. She decided to see if she could get a sandwich in the dining room.

Karyn picked up her bag and walked through the sand back toward the hotel. As she reached the main building she saw a small crowd at the far side gathered around the badminton court. Karyn strolled over to see what the attraction was. On the grassy court, under the approving eyes of the mostly middle-aged guests, Chris and Audrey were playing an energetic, laughing game of badminton. Chris wore his white trunks and a striped rugby shirt. Audrey had changed into a pale blue shorts-and-halter outfit. They were a fine-looking couple, Karyn thought unhappily. Like a travel ad in a magazine.

At that moment Audrey looked over at her. There was an unmistakable glint of triumph in her clear young eyes.

I could really learn to dislike that girl, Karyn thought, giving Audrey a bland smile in return. She left the badminton game and crossed the patch of lawn to the main building of the hotel.

From his position behind the desk in the lobby, Señor Davila, the manager, gave her a welcoming smile.

"Is it too late for me to get some lunch?" Karyn asked.

"Not at all, Señora Richter. Please go right in."

"Thank you." Karyn started for the dining room.

"Did your friend find you on the beach all right?" the manager asked.

"Mr. Halloran? Yes, he did."

Señor Davila looked puzzled. "Oh, no, señora, I mean the lady."

Karyn felt a chill. "Miss Vance?"

"No, it was your other friend. The dark lady. She asked for you and I told her you were on the beach. Is anything wrong?"

Karyn stared at him. "There was a dark woman here? Asking for me?"

The manager began to look worried. "*Sí*, señora.

Dark, with a mark of white in her hair. The lady said she was your friend. I hope I did not speak out of place."

"No—it's all right," Karyn said vaguely. She turned and started out of the building.

"Your lunch, Señora?" Davila called after her.

"I've lost my appetite," Karyn said, without looking back.

Back at the badminton court, she edged past the people who were watching, and stepped out to where Chris was preparing to serve.

"Can I talk to you?" she said.

He caught the note of urgency in her voice. "What's happened?"

"They're here. Marcia was at the desk asking for me."

Chris frowned. "When we went in to lunch there was a woman who came in a cab. She said a few words to the manager then went away."

"What did she look like?"

"Tall. Slender. Wore sunglasses. Long black hair."

"With a streak of silver?"

Chris nodded.

"That was her. I forgot that you never saw Marcia Lura. At least not as a woman."

"Damn," he said. "I was almost close enough to grab her."

The people alongside the court were watching

them curiously. Across the net Audrey stood with her fists planted on her hips.

"Can we go somewhere?" Karyn said.

"Yeah." Chris handed his racket to a paunchy man in a flowered shirt. "Here, you take over for me." He called across to Audrey, "I'll be back in a little while."

They walked away from the court together. Before she turned, Karyn caught the flash of pure female hatred in Audrey's eyes.

In a nameless *cantina* in the old Mexican section of Mazatlán, Roy Beatty sat listlessly at a table in the rear. It was dark in the *cantina*. Roy stared down at his hands, spread out flat on the sticky tabletop. He looked up at the sound of Marcia Lura's footsteps.

Marcia pulled out the chair next to him and sat down. She leaned close and spoke in an excited whisper.

"She's here."

Roy looked at her with dulled eyes, but said nothing.

"Did you hear me? I said she's here. I found her."

"I heard you."

"By now she will have been told that I asked for her at the desk. She will realize now that there is no escape for her."

Roy did not answer. Marcia reached around behind his chair. She slipped her long fingers under the hair at the back of his neck and rubbed him there.

"Don't you feel it?" she said. "This is the end of the chase."

He rolled his head around as Marcia's fingers worked on his tense trapezius muscles. "I'm glad it's almost over," he said. "That's all."

She brushed his ear with her lips. "Maybe you will feel something more when I tell you who she is with."

"Karyn is here with someone? I thought you said she came down alone."

"She did. But she met someone here."

Marcia's tongue probed at his ear, sliding in and out sensually.

Roy pushed his chair away and turned to face her. "Who? Who did she meet?"

"Your old friend, Roy, and her old lover."

"Chris Halloran? Chris is in Mazatlán?"

"You didn't think she chose this place by chance?"

"And you say they're together?"

"Oh, very much together. They're staying at the Palacio del Mar Hotel north of the city. It's very quiet there. Isolated. Perfect for lovers. And perfect for us."

Roy Beatty's lips drew back from his teeth, and for a moment the image of the wolf overlaid the man. He seemed to look out through the walls and across the city to the bed where his imagination put the naked bodies of his wife and his friend.

Marcia watched him. The corners of her wide, pale mouth lifted in a smile.

"Tonight, my Roy, we will pay them back for everything."

20

THAT EVENING CHRIS insisted that Karyn share a table with him and Audrey for dinner. Karyn was reluctant, but decided that any company, even Audrey's, was better than being alone. Her nerves had been ragged since she heard about Marcia coming to the hotel earlier in the day.

She dressed in her cabana, watching nervously through the window as the sun dropped toward the horizon. The day was still warm, but Karyn shivered as she hurried down the walk toward the main building.

Chris and Audrey were waiting for her in the dining room. Chris was unconvincingly jovial. Audrey was plainly unhappy with the situation. She wore a tight-fitting jumpsuit of simulated suede. Her hair was brushed to a coppery glow. Her eyes were continually on Karyn.

"It's so nice that you could eat with us," she said, showing her teeth.

"It's my pleasure," Karyn answered.

"No doubt," said the younger woman.

Chris cleared his throat and made a show of studying the menu. "I'm going to try the crabmeat enchiladas. How about you two?"

There was a short, uncomfortable silence. Finally Audrey said, "I want a steak. Medium well. I don't like the way they fix Mexican food down here. It's better in L.A."

"I'll just have a salad," Karyn said. She kept glancing through the archway that opened into the lobby. She could see the main entrance, and through the glass in the doors, the darkening sky outside.

"You shouldn't worry about dieting when you're on vacation," Audrey said. "So what if you do put on a few more pounds? Relax. Live a little."

Another time Karyn might have taken up the girl's challenge, but there were other things to think about. She said, "I just don't have the appetite."

"Mexico does that to some people," Audrey said. "You shouldn't have drunk the water."

Chris signaled to the waiter and ordered dinner. He tried half-heartedly to keep the conversation going, but had little success. Audrey fell into a sulk, returning her steak twice because it was not done properly. Karyn tried to follow Chris's inconsequential remarks, but her thoughts were outside where the night had once again claimed the world.

When they were finished, the waiter came and took away the empty dishes. Chris ordered sweet little Mexican cakes for dessert. Audrey found something else to complain about when she was told the kitchen was out of tea.

They dawdled over dessert until they were the last ones left in the dining room. It became plain that Chris was stalling. Audrey looked pointedly at her watch every two or three minutes.

Karyn badly wanted to leave, but she was terrified at the thought of walking alone through the dark to her cabana. She wondered how she could suggest that Chris walk with her without causing a scene with Audrey.

Before she could think of anything, Audrey spoke up. "If we're going to sit here half the night drinking this crappy coffee, I'm going to the little girl's room and at least get rid of some of it. You two *will* excuse me, I hope?"

She left the table and walked off toward the lobby, her heels ringing angrily on the tile floor.

"You'd better take me back to my room," Karyn said.

"I can't let you stay there alone," Chris said. "If Marcia was here today asking for you, it's a good bet that they'll be back tonight."

Karyn shuddered. "What can I do? I asked the manager, and there are still no rooms available in the main building. I can't sit in the lobby all night."

Chris rubbed his jaw thoughtfully. "You can come to our room."

"All night?"

"At least until we can think of something better."

"Audrey will love that."

"Audrey will have to learn that things don't always go her way."

"Have you considered telling her?"

"You mean about Drago and the werewolves?"

"Yes."

"No way. She'd laugh in my face. It's better to let her think I've got the hots for you. That's something she can understand."

"It kind of messes up your relationship, though, doesn't it?"

"That relationship is on the downslope anyway," Chris said.

Audrey came back to the table and sat down, her spirits unimproved. Karyn felt oddly guilty, as though she and Chris really did have a secret love affair going.

Audrey lifted the coffee cup to her lips, then set it down in the saucer with a thump. "I've had all this crap I can take," she announced.

Chris spoke up in a tone of artificial gaiety. "I've got an idea. Audrey, we still have that bottle of tequila that we bought at the airport. Why don't the three of us stop by for a nightcap or two?"

"Karyn's probably tired," Audrey said quickly. "Remember, she was up early this morning."

It was time, Karyn decided, to score a few points for the visiting team. "As a matter of fact, I'm not tired at all," she said, turning on a brilliant smile. "It sounds like great fun. Chris and I can talk over old times. And you and I, Audrey, can get to know each other better."

"Terrific," said Audrey.

"Fine," Chris said. "Then it's all settled."

He called for the check and signed it. They got up from the table and walked out through the archway. Passing the desk, Chris stopped.

"I just happened to think, how many glasses do we have in the room?"

"I'm sure I don't know," Audrey said.

"If I remember right, there were only two. Big water glasses." He stepped over to the desk and spoke to the manager. "Could we have some small glasses sent out to Number 7?"

Señor Davila carefully avoided looking at the two women. "Of course, Señor Halloran," he said with a professional smile. "The girl will bring them out to you."

"And send along some limes and salt," Chris added. To the women he said, "I'll show you how to drink tequila Tijuana style."

"Whoopee," said Audrey flatly.

They left the building together and walked the short distance down the path to the first cabana, the one where Chris and Audrey stayed. Chris unlocked the door and they went in. The room looked the same as Karyn's, and had been neatly tidied up by the maid. Karyn tried not to make a point of looking at the bed, though it dominated the room. Audrey walked by it deliberately and ran her hand across the spread.

Chris waved the two women to the wicker settee and pulled up the chair for himself. He carried a small table over and set it between them. From a drawer he produced a bottle of tequila. He opened the bottle and sniffed at it.

"This will be good for what ails us," he said lamely.

Audrey and Karyn looked at him without expression.

A knock on the door saved him from having to make further small talk. Blanca, the pretty young maid, came in carrying a glass bowl of fresh lime wedges and three double shot glasses along with a salt shaker.

"Now maybe the party will pick up," Chris said, forcing a laugh. He handed a bill to Blanca, who slipped it prettily down the front of her blouse.

"*Gracias,* señor," she said, with a coquettish lowering of the eyelids. With a bare flicker of a glance at Audrey and Karyn, she went out and closed the door.

Once outside, Blanca stopped and pulled the bill from its warm valley between her breasts. Five dollars, American. This was a night of good omen. And with the blond American lady busy with her friends in Number 7, it could be a beautiful night.

She hurried to a utility shed at the rear of the hotel where Roberto was busy repairing a broken chair. He looked up from his work and smiled at her.

"Can you do that later?" she said, her eyes flashing with mischief.

"Why? Now that I have started, I may as well finish the job."

"Maybe you would change your mind if I told you a secret," she said, moving close to him.

"A secret about me?"

"About us." She sat beside him on the wooden bench and ran a hand along the flank of his tight black trousers.

"Ay, girl, when you do that I have no secrets," he said.

Blanca looked down at the bulge in his pants and smiled. She brushed it with her fingertips. "Are you saving that for someone?"

"What a question, shameless girl. Take care that I do not lay you down right here where Señor Davila would surely find us."

"Would you like to make love to me now?" the girl said.

"Very much. But we have no bed. To go to your room or mine is too dangerous, and on the beach one gets sand in unmentionable places."

"We do not have to go to the beach tonight. One of the cabanas is waiting for us."

"How is that possible? No one checked out of the hotel today."

"The señora from California who arrived yesterday spends the evening with her friends in Number 7. Her cabana is at the far end, and there is no one there."

"She might return."

"Not for at least an hour. Maybe more. They have a bottle of good tequila and a bowl of limes, and the Lord knows what games in mind to keep them busy."

"Even so, she will know we have been there."

Blanca clucked her tongue impatiently. "She will know nothing. I will put fresh linen on the bed and leave the room spotless. All these objections! I think you do not really want to make love to me."

Roberto's eyes flashed. He jumped to his feet and seized Blanca's wrist, pulling her up after him. "Come along. I'll show you if I want to make love or not."

Pulling the girl behind him, he ran out of the shed, up along the side of the main building, and down the path until they came, laughing and breathing hard, to Cabana Number 12.

Blanca used her pass key to let them in. She peeled the spread, blanket, and top sheet back from the bed and folded them neatly in the chair, bending low as she did so to let the skirt ride up in back over her plump brown thighs.

She turned to face Roberto, but he had her in his arms before she could speak. His mouth found hers, and his hands raced over her body, rubbing, caressing, squeezing. After a minute they pulled apart just long enough to fumble out of their clothes and let them drop to the floor. Together they fell across the bed. Blanca opened her legs to him. With the exuberance and impatience of youth, he entered her.

At the edge of the clearing, behind the Palacio del Mar, a huge tan wolf arose from the ground where a moment before a man had writhed silently. The wolf stretched and shook, feeling the exhilarating play of its muscles. Then, leaving the pile of clothes where Roy Beatty had dropped them, the wolf moved silently through the heavy tropical growth behind the row of cabanas.

The last one in this row was the one he wanted. The windows showed no light. She would be inside asleep. Or maybe not asleep. Awake, perhaps, and staring into the darkness, fearing what she must know was somewhere outside. Soon there would be no more fear for Karyn. No more anything. The faint spark of humanity still alive in the wolf brain rebelled at the thought of the coming kill, but the dominant animal part burned with excitement.

A few yards from the cabana the wolf stopped. He raised his muzzle and tested the scent that had brought him up short. The scent of sex. Humans in rut. The wolf cocked his great head and heard the rhythmic slap-slap of naked bodies, one against the other. Belly pounding against belly as the man drove his organ into the woman.

Animal rage blazed behind the eyes of the wolf, rage fired by the memory of human jealousy. The long, sinewy legs stretched out into a loping run as the wolf closed on the cabana.

From inside came the muffled squeals and grunts of humans engaged in sex. The wolf's heart pounded in his broad chest. He would catch them together. The one-time wife and one-time friend.

With a full-throated growl, the wolf sprang from the ground and hit the window with outstretched forepaws. He took screen, frame, and glass in with him and hit the floor in a shower of splinters.

Before the two in the bed had time to react, the wolf was upon them.

Not Karyn! Nor Chris either! Strangers. A dreadful mistake, but too late, too late. The taste of blood was in the wolf's throat, and no power on earth could stop him now. In less than a minute the bed was a sopping crimson mess. Bits of flesh and hair and bone littered the floor. The wolf ripped, chewed, and swallowed, gulping the hot raw meat.

The beast growled softly as it fed, looking warily toward the window. Soon there were shouts from the main hotel building and the sound of doors opening in the other cabanas down the line. It was time to be gone.

The wolf thumped from the sodden bed to the floor. In a single graceful bound, he was back out the window and running in long fluid strides toward the forest. He was safely into the thick undergrowth by the time the first people reached the cabana.

21

THE ATMOSPHERE IN Cabana Number 7 was thick with cigarette smoke and hostility. Two of the three tequila glasses sat on the table half-full. Audrey Vance raised the third to her lips and drained it. She set it back down on the table, tipping it over as she did so.

"Lucky it wasn't full," she said. She righted the glass and poured more tequila.

"You ought to try it with lime and salt," Chris said.

"Fuck lime and salt." Audrey sniffed at the liquor, then held her glass out toward Chris. "Here's lookin' up your cucaracha."

Chris sipped at his own glass, this time forgetting

the lime himself. Karyn coughed uncomfortably and lit another cigarette.

She could not remember a more unpleasant evening. She appreciated what Chris was doing for her, and she knew she was probably safer here than in her own room, but the strain of the three-way relationship was wearing her down. She looked at her watch and saw that it was a little after midnight. A long, long time remained until dawn. The hell with this, she decided abruptly. She would go back to her own room, lock herself in, and at least would not have to put up with Audrey any more tonight.

Then there was a crash of glass, followed by screaming.

Chris stopped talking in the middle of a sentence and sat motionless for a moment. Audrey started violently, spilling tequila down the front of her blouse. Karyn stared at the darkened window. Although the screams were directionless, she was deadly certain that they came from Number 12.

"Jesus!" Audrey said. She stood up, ignoring the spilled drink. "What the hell was that?"

Chris got up and walked to the door. He opened it and stood there listening. The screams had stopped now, and there was the sound of other doors opening and questioning voices. People began running from the main building along the path that led past the cabanas. Chris started out the door.

"Don't go out there," Karyn said.

He looked back at her briefly. "I've got to see what happened."

"Then I'm coming with you," Karyn said.

"You're not going to leave me here alone," Audrey said. She walked unsteadily over and stood next to Chris, clutching his arm possessively.

For a moment Chris hesitated. They could hear voices shouting from down at the end of the row of cabanas. "All right," he said, "we'll all go. But don't get separated."

The three of them stepped out and joined the people running from the main building. There was no outside lighting along the path, and the only illumination came from the open doors of the other cabanas and several flashlights. At Number 12 the running people came to an abrupt stop. The door stood open. A man reached cautiously inside and snapped on the lights.

There was a gasp from the onlookers, and the crowd took an involuntary step backward. Audrey turned away from Chris and began to retch.

Through the open doorway Karyn caught a glimpse of the bed. Her bed. She saw what appeared to be a pile of bare human limbs on top of it. Everything was splashed a bright, wet crimson. She looked away as Chris gripped her shoulder.

Señor Davila, the hotel manager, rushed up with his thin, pale legs bare under a flannel nightshirt. He began trying simultaneously to calm the guests in English and give orders to the staff in Spanish.

The only word Karyn picked out was *policía*. Slowly the people began to move back away from the cabana as Davila selected a pair of unhappy kitchen helpers to guard the door.

Half an hour later Karyn, Chris, Audrey, and most of the other guests were gathered in the lobby of the main building. The initial shock had given way to a sort of desperate camaraderie, as with people who have shared, and survived, a disaster. On orders from Señor Davila hot coffee was being dispensed from the kitchen, and the bar, hastily reopened, was doing a booming business.

The clatter of conversation among the guests eased off as two blue and white cars with the markings of the Mazatlán police wheeled up to the front of the hotel with sirens braying.

A short, neat man in a business suit marched in at the head of several uniformed policemen. He directed the officers to their tasks, then talked quietly with Señor Davila while the guests watched with interest. After a minute he stepped to the archway between the lobby and dining room and held up a hand for attention.

"Good evening. I am Sgt. Fulgencio Vasquez of the Mazatlán Police. As you know, there has been a serious tragedy here tonight. Two employees of this hotel have been killed." He paused for a moment while the guests took in this information. "Temporary, I will use the office of Señor Davila, the manager, to do interviews. I will ask that any of you who have knowledge of this crime remain and give your name to my officer. The rest of you may return to your rooms. Please do not leave the hotel before speaking to me. Thank you for the cooperation."

There was a general stirring around among the guests. No one seemed anxious to leave.

Karyn and Chris exchanged a look. Their eyes asked, *Shall we tell?* and immediately answered, *Take care.*

There were few volunteers from among the guests to supply information, but most of them stayed around in the lobby and the bar to see what was going to happen. There was a good deal of drinking and nervous laughter as people found their quiet vacation had become an adventure.

A blue city ambulance pulled up outside, and the guests crowded out on the veranda to watch. The bodies of the two victims, strapped onto litters and covered with plastic sheets, were brought up and loaded into the back. The ambulance drove off with lights flashing and siren wailing unnecessarily.

Karyn, Chris, and Audrey sat on a wood and leather sofa on one side of the lobby and watched the others jostle for a look at the departing ambulance.

"They act like it's a holiday of some kind," Karyn said.

"It's a touch of hysteria," Chris said. "What

they're saying inside is, 'Thank God it happened to somebody else and not me.' "

Karyn shivered. Chris reached over and squeezed her hand.

"I've got a fucking headache that won't quit," Audrey said.

"Do you want to go back to the room?" Chris asked.

"Not by myself, I don't."

"I'll go see if I can get you some aspirin."

Chris started to rise, but sat back down when he saw Sergeant Vasquez coming toward them across the lobby. The policeman stopped before the sofa and nodded politely. He focused his attention on Karyn.

"Mrs. Richter?"

"Yes?"

"I am told it was in your cabana that this unfortunate tragedy took place."

"Yes, it was."

"Will you be good enough to come into the office?"

Karyn looked questioningly at Chris.

He said, "Is it all right if I come along, Sergeant? I'm a friend of Mrs. Richter."

Vasquez's cool brown eyes took in the two of them. "A friend, you say?"

"That's right. We knew each other back in the States."

"Don't mind me," Audrey said. "I'm just passing through."

Vasquez gave her a chilly smile. To Chris he said, "I have no objection if you wish to come."

Chris turned to Audrey. "This shouldn't take too long."

"What the hell, take all the time you want," Audrey said. "I'll be in the bar."

Chris patted her knee and smiled. She turned away. He shrugged and joined Karyn and Sergeant Vasquez as they crossed the lobby to enter the small office tucked in behind the registration desk.

Vasquez put them into hard-backed chairs facing him as he sat behind a small desk. He offered his pack of Mexican cigarettes and took one for himself when they both declined. He inhaled deeply, then leaned forward across the desk and fixed them with a steady brown gaze.

"The two of you were together this evening?"

"That's right," Chris answered. "Miss Vance was with us."

"Ah, yes, the young lady in the lobby."

Chris nodded.

Vasquez regarded him for a moment without expression, then he turned to Karyn.

"Mrs. Richter, do you know of anyone who might want to kill you?"

"Me?"

"The young people were murdered in your room.

The lights were out. It is possible that the killer was after you and did not see his mistake until it was too late."

"I just arrived in Mazatlán," Karyn said carefully. "I don't know anyone here, except Mr. Halloran."

"Ah, yes." The policeman switched his attention to Chris. "And you, sir, have you any opinions about this tragedy?"

"I don't know any more than Mrs. Richter," Chris said.

Vasquez held Chris for a long moment with his somber gaze, then turned it on Karyn. When neither of them reacted the sergeant relaxed a little and gave them a cool smile. "It was just a thought. The truth is we are fairly certain who the killer is, but I do not wish to overlook other possibilities."

"You know who did it?" Chris said.

"In a crime of passion such as this, we look first for the husband. In this case we have no husband, but we do have a former lover of the girl. A man given to violent acts, I am told. He worked here at the hotel and was discharged a month ago."

Karyn bit her lip. "Are you certain this was done by a man?"

"It is not a woman's crime, señora," said Vasquez.

"That's not what I meant."

"Oh?" The policeman assumed an expression of polite attention.

Karyn felt her face growing warm. She looked to Chris for help, but he gave her only a tiny shake of his head. "I just wondered," she said, "whether it could have been—an animal."

"Impossible," the policeman said at once. "I do not wish to make light of your suggestion, señora, but there is no animal capable of doing what was done to those two young people."

A uniformed policeman entered the office. He looked quickly at Karyn and Chris, then spoke to Vasquez. *"Con perdón . . ."*

"Qué?"

The policeman spoke rapidly in Spanish as Vasquez listened and nodded. The man placed an envelope on the desk in front of the sergeant as he spoke. Vasquez opened it and peered inside. From a pocket he produced a pair of tweezers, which he used to withdraw the contents of the envelope. He held it up to the light and examined it, then set it down carefully on the desk. A thick tuft of coarse tan fur. He said something to the man in uniform, who saluted and went out.

"It seems the killer left something behind when he went out the window," said Vasquez. He picked up the tuft of fur again in the tweezers and displayed it proudly, like it was a rare butterfly. "One of the men found this caught on the torn window screen."

Karyn and Chris stared at the bit of fur. Neither of them spoke.

Vasquez smiled thinly at Karyn. "I'm sure it is not what you think, señora. Torn from a fur-lined jacket, I would guess. It will be most helpful when we pick up our man."

Karyn started to speak, but caught a warning glance from Chris, and held back.

"There is something, señora?" said Vasquez.

Karyn shook her head. "No, nothing. Is it all right if we go now?"

"Yes, of course. Thank you both for your time."

They walked out of the manager's office and across the lobby. Most of the guests by this time had drifted off to their rooms.

"We can't let them arrest an innocent man," Karyn said.

"What do you suggest? Going up to Sergeant Vasquez and saying, 'Hey, I think those people were killed by a werewolf who used to be my husband'?"

"Please don't be sarcastic."

Chris passed a hand over his brow. "I'm sorry. Getting tired, I guess. But I don't think you have to worry about an innocent man being locked up. Despite what you might have read, the Mexican system of criminal justice is reasonably competent."

"I suppose so," Karyn said wearily. "And you're right. There really is nothing we could do." Without warning she yawned.

"We'd all better get some sleep," Chris said.

"Let's find the manager and arrange for a room for you."

Señor Davila, now fully dressed, but still unshaven, said yes, a room in the main building could be made ready at once for Señora Richter, since a number of guests had suddenly checked out.

As Karyn filled out a new registration card, Chris snapped his fingers.

"Damn, I forgot about Audrey. She's still waiting in the bar."

"You'd better go and get her," Karyn said. "I can handle things from here on."

"I'll see you first thing in the morning," Chris said. He hurried away toward the bar.

Karyn finished signing in for the new room while Señor Davila sent a boy out to see about bringing her things in from Cabana 12. She sat down in a chair in the lobby to wait, and massaged her eyes.

"Señora?"

She looked up, and for a moment could not place the stocky man with the luxuriant moustache who had spoken.

"Luis Zarate?" he said with a rising inflection. "The taxi from the airport yesterday?"

"Oh, yes," Karyn said. She waited for the man to speak.

"If the señora will permit, I think I can be of assistance."

"Thank you, but I won't be needing a taxi tonight."

"No, señora, not a taxi, but you do need help, maybe, I think."

"What do you mean?"

"The young Blanca, and her *novio*, Roberto, they died tonight, I think, in your place."

"How do you know this?" Karyn asked. She watched the man intently.

"There is much I know. Remember, I told you I have gypsy blood. I know it was no man who killed Roberto and Blanca."

"Who, then?"

"Not *who*, señora, *what*. These killings carry the mark of *lobombre*. The werewolf."

22

IN THE PART OF Mazatlán away from the sparkling beaches and bright new streets was a section of the city called La Ratonera, the rathole. It was a neighborhood where the sightseeing buses never came, and only a foolhardy tourist ventured. The streets were cracked and pitted, the buildings crusted with the filth of decades. Doors were always closed, windows covered. The air was heavy with the smell of human feces and human despair.

From La Ratonera came the used-up prostitutes, the burned-out thieves, the hopeless drunkards and the dying dopers. At night they moved like shadows along the broken streets, in the light of day they shut themselves inside.

Here, in a musty room behind a nameless *cantina,*

Roy Beatty lay face down on the thin mattress of a rusted iron bed. The wallpaper of the room had long ago peeled away to the brown-stained plaster. Vermin scuttled through piles of debris in the corner.

Marcia Lura stood with her arms folded, looking down at Roy. She was oblivious to the squalor around her. The grace of her body and her fierce beauty made her seem an alien being in this lowly place. The green fires in her eyes snapped with suppressed rage.

"You failed again," she said. Her voice was low and vibrant like a taut cello string. "Three times now you have set out to kill, and three times you have blundered. First there was the boy in Seattle. Simple enough, but instead of him, you killed a useless old woman. Then in Los Angeles you had a chance at your Karyn, but you let her get away. And now you have missed her again. After last night she will be more on her guard than ever, and it will be still more difficult for us."

Roy groaned softly where he lay, but did not turn his head to look at her.

"You know that I have to rely on you," Marcia went on. "I would give anything if it were possible for me to make the kill. You know that. And you know why I cannot. I have put all my faith in you, Roy, and you have failed me. Not once, but three times."

"Enough!"

Marcia started, shocked by the unexpected strength in Roy's voice. He sat up in the bed and faced her.

"I don't want to hear any more about failure," he said. "Two young people died last night. Two people who had done you no harm. Nor me. And yet I killed them. With the woman in Seattle, that makes three. Three innocent people I have killed for you."

Marcia's eyes met his, and she slowly recovered her poise. It was Roy who looked away first.

"You killed them for me, did you?" Her voice was dangerously soft. "Just for me. Look at me, Roy. Tell me you did not enjoy the killing. Tell me you did not exult in the power of your muscles as you ripped the throat from the old woman who foolishly stood in your way. Tell me that as you savaged the naked bodies of the couple on the bed that you did not feel a sexual thrill of your own. Can you tell me this?"

Roy's gaze returned to her, but when he spoke much of the power was gone from his voice. "No, I can't deny those things. Because of what I am, the killing excites me. I need it. But because what I used to be, it disgusts me."

Marcia walked to the bed. She sat next to Roy on the threadbare mattress and eased his head down onto her large, firm breasts.

"I know the pain you feel, my Roy," she said. "I understand. As the time passes, the pain will grow less. One day all memories of the man you were—that weak, shallow, ignorant man—will fade to shadows. You will glory in what you are. The strength of the wolf will be your joy, and you will know only joy. Then you and I will truly be together. That is what you want, isn't it, my Roy?"

"Yes." His words were muffled against the silk of her blouse. "That's what I want."

Gently Marcia opened the buttons down the front of her blouse, freeing her breasts. They glowed pale and smooth in the faint light that filtered into the room. Roy took her nipple into his mouth. She stroked the shaggy blond hair at the back of his head and spoke in a low, caressing tone.

"Our mission here will soon be ended. Time is short for us now because the woman has an ally. Her lover, your one-time friend. We must separate them. Together they are dangerous because they know what they are fighting. They know our strength, and will not be taken by surprise."

She was silent for a moment and pressed Roy's head tight against her. "And worse, they know our weakness."

Roy brushed his lips over the upper curve of her breast and kissed the ivory-smooth throat. He pulled back from her and reached out to touch the silver streak in her hair.

"My poor Marcia," he murmured. "They hurt you so."

The blazing green eyes stared into the past.

"Never will I forget the pain of that silver bullet. There is no pain to compare."

"I promise they will pay for that," Roy said. "I won't fail you again."

Marcia stroked his broad back. Her fingers caressed the smooth, powerful muscles. "I know you won't," she said. "But it will be difficult. They will seek help against us."

"How can we stop them?"

"There are many gypsies in Mazatlán, people who have come down from the mountains. People who remember the old laws. We will spread the word among them. We cannot allow the woman and her lover to arm themselves against us as they did before. We must strike first."

"Will the gypsies help us?"

"We don't need their help. All we will ask of the gypsies is that they give no help to our enemies. They will not deny us that. They will not act against *lobombre*."

Roy's body tensed, but he began to relax as Marcia used her fingers on him, then her mouth. In a little while there was no more rebellion in him.

23

IN THE MORNING AFTER the bloody business in Cabana 12, the sun had barely cleared the mountains behind the Palacio del Mar, but the grounds and the lobby were alive with people. There were members of the Mazatlán police force along with people from the State of Sinaloa and the Mexican government. The sightseers had not started to arrive yet, since the morning papers were not out with the news.

At a table in the dining room, Karyn sat over sweet rolls and coffee with Chris Halloran and a worried-looking Luis Zarate. They looked around furtively, like conspirators, and talked in low, guarded voices.

"I understand you said last night you could help us," Chris said.

Luis' eyes darted around the room. "I did not say that exactly."

"Well, what exactly *did* you say?"

"What I was going to say is that I know somebody who maybe can help you."

"Damn it, man, get on with it. Do we have to drag every word out of you?"

Karyn laid a hand on Chris's arm. "Please, Chris, let Luis tell us in his own way."

"*Gracias,* señora," said the taxi driver. "The one I know, the one who may help you, lives in the mountains back of the city of Mazatlán. She is a gypsy. Very old. Her name is Philina."

"What the hell good is an old gypsy lady going to do us?" Chris demanded. "We're talking about werewolves, not tea leaves. I thought you understood that."

Luis pushed his chair back from the table. With as much dignity as he could summon, he started to rise. "If the señor is not interested, I will take no more of your time."

"Please, Luis, sit down," Karyn said. "We want very much to hear what you have to say." She frowned at Chris.

"I'm sorry, Luis," he said. "I'm just upset. We don't want any more people to die. And we need all the help we can get, from anyone who will give it. I truly appreciate your offer."

Luis eased back into the chair. "*Muy bien.* Philina is, like I told you, a very old gypsy. She is full-blooded gypsy, not just little part like me." He blinked a smile on and off, then continued. "Philina sees things in your hand. She knows things that are going to happen. If there is anyone who can help you fight *lobombre,* it is Philina the gypsy."

"Can you take us to her?" Karyn asked.

"I can take you some of the way—as far as the road goes. After that there is a mountain trail that leads to her cabin."

"That's no good," Chris said. "We haven't time to go hunting through strange mountain country for some old woman. If we are caught out after dark, we'll be at the mercy of the werewolves."

"The journey can be made in the daylight hours if one starts early," said Luis. "I have a cousin who lives at the end of the road. He keeps burros for mountain travelers. He will let you have two of them for a small price. The burros know the way up the trail. It is the only one leading up the mountain."

"If we started now, could we make it today before dark?" Karyn asked.

Luis glanced through the window, checking the angle of the sun. He nodded.

Karyn and Chris looked at each other. "What do you think?" she said.

"To tell you the truth, I think it's a waste of time. I can't see what good an old gypsy fortuneteller can do us."

"Chris, we have nothing else."

"But palm-reading. Do you believe in that?"

"Do you believe in werewolves?" Karyn said quietly.

"Touché," said Chris.

"Even if the old woman can do nothing for us, all we've lost is one day. And it's just possible that she's for real, and can somehow help us. I think it's worth trying."

Chris rubbed his jaw thoughtfully. "Okay," he said. "I'm game if you are." And to Luis: "How soon can you be ready to go?"

"I am ready now, señor. My taxi is parked just outside."

"Good. Karyn, I think it would be best if you stay here while I go check out the gypsy lady."

"Not a chance," Karyn said. "I'm going with you." When Chris started to protest she held up a hand to stop him. "Please don't go all macho and protective on me. This is more my fight than it is yours, and I'm not going to sit in my room wringing my hands while you're out doing things."

"All right then," Chris said reluctantly, "we'll both go. While you put on something suitable for burro-riding, I'll go try to head off trouble with Audrey."

Audrey Vance sat up in the bed and held the sheet wrapped tight around her lithe body as she listened to Chris tell her he was going to leave her this morning. Her gray eyes were like chips of granite.

"I know this isn't a lot of fun for you," he said, "but please believe me when I tell you it's super-important."

Audrey stared at him coldly before answering. "And you have to be gone all day."

"Most of it, probably."

"With your ex-girlfriend."

"Karyn is not my ex-girlfriend."

"Whatever the hell you want to call her, then."

Chris sighed heavily. "Yes, Karyn will be with me."

"Very cozy."

"I can't help what you think."

Audrey turned away, letting him see her best profile. "Maybe it would be better if I just went back to Los Angeles alone."

After a moment Chris said, "As a matter of fact, that might be the best thing to do."

Audrey turned toward him quickly. She reached out her arms, letting the sheet fall away from her high, firm breasts. "I didn't mean it, Chris. I don't want to go back without you. Look at me, I promised you I'd never be jealous, and here I am doing exactly that. Look, if you've got something important you have to do with the woman, go ahead. I'll find something around here to keep me busy today."

Chris relaxed. He placed his hands flat against the girl's sides, feeling the ribs outlined under the firm flesh. "Thanks, honey. I'll tell you all about it some time when there's no pressure. If I tried to explain it now, take my word for it, you wouldn't believe me."

Audrey locked her hands behind his head and tried to pull him down with her on the bed. "At least you can leave me with a little something to think about."

He held himself back. "Sorry, honey, I just haven't got the time."

She released her hold immediately and looked up into his eyes. Little white tension lines appeared at the corners of her mouth. "Jesus, thanks a lot."

Chris tried a smile. "When I go to bed with you, I want us to have time to do it right. You don't want to start knocking off quickies, do you?"

"Just go on and do whatever you have to do." Audrey gathered the sheet around her again. "I'll see you when you get back."

Chris stood for a moment looking at her. When she would not meet his eye he went out and closed the door firmly behind him.

Karyn was waiting on the veranda with Luis when Chris returned. She had changed into a pair of jeans and a light-weight jacket over a sweater.

"How did it go?" she said.

"Not too good."

"I'm sorry."

"Don't worry about it. That's my problem."

As they started down the steps Karyn touched Chris's arm. "There's that policeman who talked to us last night. I want to see him for a minute."

She walked up the path to where Sergeant Vasquez stood talking to a young uniformed policeman, who nodded several times, then hurried off.

"Excuse me, Sergeant," Karyn said.

"Señora Richter, good morning."

"I was wondering—you said last night that there was this friend of the girl, the one who was killed, who you thought might have done it—"

Vasquez raised his hands in a helpless gesture. "Unfortunately for us, the young man has the perfect alibi. For the past seven days, including last night, he has been locked in jail in Culiacán."

Karyn fought to suppress a smile of relief. "I see. Well, I was just wondering. Thank you."

She hurried back to rejoin Chris and Luis Zarate. They climbed into the taxi and rolled away from the hotel toward Mazatlán. Before they reached the city, Luis turned off the highway onto a narrow, unpaved road that led off into the foothills of the Occidental Mountains.

Once they were away from the cooling effect of the sea breeze, the air in the car became hot and steamy. Opening the windows did no good. However, it began to cool off again as the road started to climb.

The rutted road finally came to an end at a pile of boulders. Luis eased the car off into the gravel in front of a weathered shack built of lumber scraps and flattened tin cans. He honked the horn steadily until a swarthy man, with a limp and one clouded eye, came out of the shack. Luis got out of the car and spoke to him in Spanish while Karyn and Chris stood by waiting. Finally Luis rejoined them.

"My cousin Guillermo will let you have two burros for the day for ten dollars. It is too much, but he knows you are Americans, and to ignorant peons like Guillermo all Americans are very rich."

"Tell him it's a deal," Chris said.

Luis passed the word to his cousin, and the man limped back behind the shack and returned a minute later leading two sleepy burros that looked as if the moths had been at them.

"Are you sure they'll make it up the mountain?" Chris said.

"Estos es muy buenos burros," said Guillermo, catching the tone of Chris's voice, if not the meaning of his words. *"Muy robustos."*

"Yeah, I'll bet," Chris muttered.

"What about saddles?" Karyn asked.

Guillermo looked blank.

She patted the seat of her jeans, then the bony back of one of the burros. "Saddle," she repeated.

A light came into Guillermo's good eye. "Oh, *sí, las mantas!*" He limped into the shack and returned with two thin, tattered blankets. He folded them carefully and lay them over the backs of the burros.

"Swell," Karyn said. She glanced over at Luis.

"Don't worry," he said. "These burros do not move fast enough to throw you off." ◂

"That's not what I'm worried about," Karyn said drily.

"We'd better get started," Chris said. "Which one do you want?"

Karyn looked the two animals over. They were about the same size, and their gentle, sleepy eyes told her nothing. She rubbed the ruff of hair between the ears of one of them. The burro did not move.

"I like this one," she said. "He's got spirit."

With help from Luis and his cousin, they climbed aboard the animals. Guillermo showed them how to hold onto the rope that was attached to a simple bit in each burro's mouth.

"You're sure we'll be able to find the place all right?" Chris said.

"The burros will take you there," Luis assured him. "They will follow the trail, and the trail leads only to the gypsy."

"And you'll meet us here when we come down?" Karyn said.

"*Sí*, señora. I will be waiting a full two hours before sundown. Take care you are not caught in the darkness. Night comes quickly in these mountains."

"Don't worry," Karyn told him, "we won't take any chances."

They clucked to the burros, and with a little urging the animals started off at a slow, patient pace up the rocky trail that led into the mountains.

Karyn soon found that riding burro-back was every bit as uncomfortable as she had imagined. In less than half an hour the insides of her thighs were chafed raw, and her buttocks ached from the steady jolting gait of the beasts.

Chris, riding ahead on the narrow trail, turned back. "How you doing?"

"Just great, but I may never sit down again."

After riding up the ever-steepening grade for more than another hour, they came to a clearwater spring that bubbled out between two rocks. Karyn and Chris dismounted gratefully and drank deeply of the icy water while the burros dipped their muzzles in the pool downstream.

"How about a short rest?" Chris said.

"I'd appreciate it."

Chris sat down on a rock among the scrubby chapparal that grew along the trail. Karyn eased into a semi-reclining position beside him.

"I sure hope this trip is worth the aches and pains," she said.

Chris grinned at her. "I was willing to come up alone, remember?"

"Come on, cowboy, let's ride," she said, pushing painfully to her feet.

Chuckling, Chris remounted his burro and they set off again.

The sun had passed its zenith when they topped the first crest. On the other side the trail dipped down sharply into a steep valley of tangled green rain forest.

"God, how much farther can it be?" Karyn said.

"I think this is it," Chris said. "Look over there."

Karyn followed his pointing finger and saw, just over the rise of ground, the top of a cabin. The walls were unfinished logs, the roof a heavy thatch of dry grass. From a hole in the roof a trail of gray smoke drifted into the air. The cabin had an unreal, fairy-tale look.

"The house of the wicked witch," Karyn said, and immediately wished she hadn't.

They got down off the burros and tied them loosely to a clump of chapparal, undoing the rope bits so they could eat. The docile animals lowered their heads and began to chew on the coarse grass.

Karyn and Chris approached the hut together. There was no door. Instead, the heavy tanned hide of some animal hung across the opening. From inside came the smell of something gamy cooking.

"Hello?" Chris called at the door. "Anybody here?"

No answer.

Chris looked at Karyn with a shrug, then drew aside the hide covering the doorway. The smell of cooking, new and old, hit them like a fist. In the center of the single room a low fire burned in a pit lined with rocks. Over the flame, a blackened five-gallon can was suspended on a pole. Something bubbled sluggishly in the can. The room was oppressively hot.

"Váyase. Go away."

For a moment Karyn could not locate the source of the voice. Then, as her eyes adjusted to the gloom inside the cabin, she saw a tall woman, thin as a stick, with straight white hair and a black dress that had been patched many times. The woman stood on the other side of the fire pit, looking at them.

"Luis Zarate told us to come to you," Chris said. He squinted into the shadows, trying to get a clear look at the woman.

The gypsy took a step toward them. The glow from the fire accentuated the highlights and shadows of her face. Her nose was thin and highly arched. The cheekbones stood out prominently over the deep hollows of her cheeks. Her skin was leathery and wrinkled, but in the dark fiery eyes was a hint of the wild beauty she once had been. She fixed them with a steady gaze, Chris first, then Karyn.

"You are the ones, then," she said. Her voice was steady and ageless.

"Luis spoke to you about us?" Karyn said.

"I have not seen him."

"You said—we are the ones."

"I knew you were coming."

"Can we speak to you?" Chris said, his tone automatically respectful.

"Ah, well, come inside if you must," the old woman said.

Karyn and Chris entered the dark interior of the cabin. There was no carpet on the hard dirt floor, and little furniture that was recognizable. When Chris let the hide fall back over the doorway, the only light came from the fire.

The gypsy, Philina, motioned Karyn into an old wooden chair that had no back. Chris stood beside her. The old woman sat down on a pile of rags facing them. She drew her legs up and crossed them beneath her.

"Tell me your story," Philina said.

Karyn began to talk, haltingly at first, then more freely. She told the old woman about the things that had happened to her, beginning with her first encounter with the werewolves in the California village of Drago. She talked about the renewal of the horror this summer in Seattle, and how it followed her to her parents' home in Los Angeles, and finally here to the west coast of Mexico.

The old gypsy listened silently. She did not move or change her expression. The only sign that she was not asleep was the glitter of her eyes in the firelight.

When Karyn had finished there was no sound in the cabin for a long time. At last Philina spoke. "So you have come to me."

"Yes," Karyn said. "Can you help us?"

Philina gazed into the fire for such a long time, Karyn began to think she *had* fallen asleep. Then abruptly she looked up and said, "Let me see your hand."

Karyn glanced at Chris, then rose and walked over to where the gypsy was sitting. She knelt next to the old woman and held out her hand. Philina took it in her own bony fingers. There was surprising strength in her hand. She traced the lines with a cracked fingernail, muttering to herself in a language Karyn did not recognize.

After a few minutes the gypsy released Karyn's hand and turned to Chris. "Now yours."

Chris came over and offered his palm. Philina scanned the lines briefly, then dropped his hand.

"I cannot help you," she said.

"What did you see?" Karyn asked.

Philina looked up. The shadows thrown by the dull red fire made her face skull-like. "Sometimes it is better not to know."

"For God's sake, let's hear it," Chris said. He took out his wallet and began thumbing through the bills. "I'll pay you. How much do you want?"

The old woman made a dry sound in her throat that might have been laughter. "Your money is of no use to me. If you insist on knowing, sit down and I will tell you what I saw in your hands. But do not blame me afterwards."

With a gesture of impatience Chris put away his wallet. He went back and sat on the broken chair. Karyn stayed where she was next to the old woman.

Philina paused, looking again into the fire before she spoke. "I need give only one reading for the two of you, for I see the same thing in the hands. I see pain. And blood. Much blood. And death."

"No!" The word was out before Karyn could think.

The old woman looked at her sharply. "What did you come looking for, some carnival trickster? Did you expect me to tell you of long, happy sea voyages and surprise gifts of money? Of romantic strangers entering your lives? Bah! You asked me what I saw in your hands. I have told you. Now go."

Chris stood up, but said nothing. He helped Karyn to her feet.

"Is there nothing we can do?" Karyn said.

"Arm yourselves as you did once before," the Gypsy answered. "Then you may have a chance."

"Is there no place we can be safe?"

The gypsy shook her head slowly. "There is no place. Your destiny is here, and you cannot run away from it. It is here that your story must end."

"End?" Chris said sharply. "What do you mean end? End how?"

The old woman returned to staring at the fire. She said nothing.

"Chris, what's the time?" Karyn said suddenly.

He glanced at his watch, then strode to the doorway and pulled aside the animal skin. The sun had moved markedly toward the horizon. The valley to the east of the gypsy's cabin was already in shadow.

"It's time to go," he said.

Karyn crossed the room and joined him at the doorway. Philina remained sitting on the pile of rags, not looking at them. Chris pulled two bills from his wallet and held them out toward the old woman. She made no move to take the money. Chris laid the bills on the broken chair, and with Karyn beside him left the cabin.

The journey down the mountain trail was much swifter than coming up. The burros, knowing they were headed home, jogged along at a spine-jarring rate. Still, the sun seemed to plunge ahead of them. By the time they reached the shack of Guillermo the burro-keeper, it was twilight. Behind them the mountain loomed black and forbidding.

Karyn was vastly relieved to see Luis waiting there for them in his battered taxi. She and Chris quickly dismounted and turned the burros over to Guillermo. They hurried to the car and got in, automatically locking the doors and rolling the windows up tight. Luis gunned the Plymouth down the dirt road toward the highway and the city.

"We did cut it a little close," Chris said.

Karyn turned to look out the rear window. "Yes, for a minute there I thought—"

She left the sentence unfinished, for from somewhere back there in the dark, tangled chaparral came the howling.

24

ROY BEATTY CROUCHED in the brush alongside the road and watched as his wife and his friend
climbed into the battered taxi. They were not thirty
yards away from him. How open they would be at
this moment, how vulnerable to the attack of the
wolf! Roy looked anxiously off to the west. The
sun was almost down, but enough glowing red
showed at the horizon to prevent him from chang-
ing. Enough to save the lives of these two people.
This time.

The shadows of the twilight lengthened and
joined and spread like ink spilled from a bottle until
there was darkness. Roy tore the soft cotton shirt
from his back. He pulled off the canvas shoes he
wore over bare feet, and stepped out of his pants.

He knelt naked in the fast-chilling night and willed his body to change.

His muscles bunched and released convulsively. His joints cracked audibly as the bones shifted in their sockets. He fell forward to his hands and knees. His neck arched. There was an instant of blinding pain as the change wracked his body. Then came the exultation. The wild joy of freedom as the great tan wolf took possession of the man.

The wolf moved silently out from behind the brush. The head turned and the yellow eyes looked off down the rutted dirt road that wound down toward the highway. Far below, the glowing red tail lights of the taxi were still visible. The wolf raised his muzzle to the night sky and howled—a cry of hate and defiance.

In the enclosure behind the shack of Guillermo, the burros twitched their ears at the sound. They looked up from their grazing and stirred restlessly. In their soft, drowsy eyes was the shadow of fear.

The door of the cabin opened the width of a hand and Guillermo looked out. He saw nothing in the night, and quickly withdrew. There was the sound of heavy scraping from within as Guillermo moved things against the door to keep out the evil.

Deep in his throat the wolf growled softly. How futile would be the burro-keeper's attempt to bar the door if the wolf really wanted to get in. Against the werewolf the flimsy shack would offer no more protection than a house of paper. But Guillermo was safe this night. He was of no importance; he knew nothing. But there was another in these mountains who would not be so lucky. One who must learn the price of betrayal. The wolf turned and started up the mountain.

The fire burned low, and then it died to glowing coals in the cabin of Philina the gypsy. She sat still in the cross-legged position she had been in when the man and the woman were here. The money the man had left lay untouched and unseen on the broken chair. Although the night grew cold, the old woman made no move to rebuild the dying fire. She knew she would not need it.

She had lived many years, Philina. How many was it? Eighty? Ninety? She could not remember. She did remember that once in the long dead past she had been a young girl. A beautiful, laughing young girl. The bloodless lips of the old woman moved in a faint, bitter smile. How long had it been since anyone might have believed that once she was beautiful? Or young?

And yet it had been so. In a village near Torrelavega, where the Cantabrian Mountains came down to meet the Bay of Biscay, the young Philina had laughed and danced and sang and flirted with the boys like any Spanish gypsy girl. Then abruptly it had all ended. The gypsies discovered that she had The Gift.

The Gift! The old woman made a rattling sound

in her throat. The *Curse* would be closer to the truth. The Curse of Prophecy. When it became known that she could read what was in the hands, girlhood was over for Philina. The people either clamored after her, begging for a reading, or they shunned her to avoid one. She no longer had friends. And the young men who courted her wanted only to use her terrible power.

In the end she had fled from all of them and crossed the ocean to live by herself. She chose the mountains above Mazatlán because it reminded her of her home in Spain, where she had known her only happiness, for such a short time.

But of course she could not forever conceal The Gift. There were gypsies here, too, and they knew at once. Philina never went into the city, and she discouraged all who would come to her cabin, but still they sought her out. There were not so many now as in the early years, but still some came, like the two young Americans today. They would be the last.

The Gift. In how many hands over the years had she read the future? Happiness, grief, riches, pain, births, illness, and death. She had seen it all. To Philina the gypsy, all hands were windows to the future. All hands, save her own. Some merciful power withheld from those cursed with The Gift that one ability that might drive them mad—the ability to read their own futures.

And yet now Philina knew what lay ahead for

her. She knew how short was the time she had left. Minutes. She had read it in the hands of the two young strangers. They had brought her death. They had done so innocently, but they had brought death as surely as though they had plunged a knife into her heart.

The old woman sighed. She was ready. She had lived a long time, and there was nothing left undone.

She heard death coming outside. It moved softly through the grass of the clearing before her cabin. Over the years Philina's sight had dimmed, but her ears were as keen as ever. She heard the snuffling sound as death approached. It stopped just outside her doorway, and she could hear the air rush in and out of its powerful lungs. Still the gypsy made no move.

The hide that covered the doorway was torn away as the wolf burst through. It hesitated a moment, snarling, feet braced on the hard dirt floor. Then it sprang.

Philina made no attempt to protect herself from the murderous teeth. It would have been no use anyway. She had lived a long time, and she was ready.

25

BY THE FOLLOWING morning the news of the double murder had been widely reported, and the Palacio del Mar Hotel had become famous. Sightseers streamed in from Mazatlán, Culiacán, Durango, and even La Paz across the Gulf of California for a look at the *"cabana de muerte,"* as the newspapers were calling Number 12. Taxis came and left in a steady procession, and at least one tour bus had been rerouted to include the Palacio.

There were still police on the scene, and along with the reporters and curiosity seekers, they gave a sense of great excitement to the normally quiet hotel. Señor Davila, the manager, apologized profusely to the regular guests for the inconvenience, but he was enterprising enough to hire extra help for the bar and double the size of the souvenir stand in the lobby.

The dining room that morning was the only part of the hotel that was relatively uncrowded. It was there that Karyn and Chris sat at a small table, talking in low, tense voices.

Chris leaned forward, ignoring the muddy coffee cooling in a cup before him. "If anybody had told me three years ago that one day I would be making plans based on the ravings of a gypsy fortuneteller, I'd have laughed in his face."

"But it's different now," Karyn said.

"A lot of things are different now."

"So what's our next move?"

"The gypsy said we had a chance if we arm ourselves as we did before."

"How can we do that, Chris? You don't have a gun here, do you?"

"No. And for a foreigner, it's just about impossible to get one. Let alone silver bullets. But the only things we have to fight them with is fire and silver. We can't control fire, so it will have to be a silver weapon of some kind. A knife, maybe."

"Can you get a silver knife?"

"I've got to. There's not much time. Did you check the calendar?"

"Yes. Tonight is the full moon."

"If the gypsy woman was right, and we might as well assume she was, then tonight it all comes to an end."

"One way or another," Karyn said.

"Right. One way or another."

There was an awkward pause. Chris looked at his watch. "I'd better get into town and see about the knife. While I'm gone, it might be best if you stayed in your room."

"No," Karyn said.

Chris looked up sharply. "What?"

"I'm not going to lock myself in like some frightened child. Let me go with you."

Chris shook his head. "I can move faster alone."

"All right, but I have to do something besides sit here."

He saw the look in her eye and relented. "At least don't go off anywhere by yourself."

"Maybe I'll take the cruise in the glass-bottomed boat. How would that be?"

"I'd feel a lot easier if you stayed locked in your room."

"There's nothing to worry about. I'll be with twenty other people. The boat leaves before noon and doesn't stay out more than an hour or so. That will get me back well before dark."

"I hope I'm back well before dark too," Chris said. "I'll make it as fast as I can. We'll stay together tonight and hope that the gypsy was right— that this will be the end of it."

"What about Audrey?"

"I don't have time to worry about Audrey's hurt feelings any more. She'll just have to do the best she can." He pushed away from the table and stood up. "I've got to get started. See you."

"See you, Chris. Take care of yourself."

"You too." He squeezed her shoulder and went out, quickly disappearing in the crowd of people in the lobby.

Audrey was still in bed when Chris returned to the cabana. She lay on her stomach with her head turned to one side. Her skin was pale, and there was a film of perspiration on her forehead. The flesh under her eyes was faintly purple.

"How do you feel?" Chris asked as he crossed to the closet.

"Like death. What the hell is that Mexican booze made out of, anyway?"

"Cactus."

"I believe it." Groaning, she sat up in bed and watched Chris pull on a jacket. "Where are you going?"

"Into town."

"What do we have to do in town?"

"Not 'we,' *me.*"

"You're going to leave me here alone again?"

"That's right."

Audrey threw back the sheet and got out of bed. She was still wearing the blue bikini panties she hadn't taken off the night before. She stood before Chris swaying slightly. The color surged back into her face.

"What the hell is going on, anyway?" she demanded. "You invite me to spend a couple of weeks in Mexico with you, then you let me sit around this fucking room drinking this foul Mexican booze while you cozy it up with your old lady friend and go off on mysterious trips and—" Anger rose in her throat and choked off the words.

"Go back to bed," Chris said without looking at her. "The rest will do you good."

"Like hell I will. I'm not going to take this shit from you any more."

Chris turned to face her squarely. "Audrey, you don't have to take anything. Our return tickets to Los Angeles are in the top of my suitcase. You can use yours any time you want to."

Audrey caught her breath. She moved in quickly and wrapped her arms around him.

"I'm sorry, Chris, I didn't mean all that. I'm just hung over. I miss you, that's all. I want to be with you."

He held her for a moment. "I'm sorry, too. I didn't intend it to be this way. Things have come up that I don't have any control over."

"Can't you tell me about it?"

"Not now." He pulled away from her gently. "I've got to go."

Audrey released him. He kissed her lightly and went out.

Chris walked along in front of the hotel, where the driveway was crowded with vehicles bringing sightseers from Mazatlán. Halfway down the line he spotted the battered Plymouth of Luis Zarate. He hurried over and leaned down at the open window on the driver's side.

"Luis, can you take me into town?"

The cab driver looked up, startled. "Oh, señor, *buenas días*. I was, ah, waiting for a passenger."

"I'm a passenger." Chris opened the back door and got in. "Let's go."

Luis sighed heavily and started the noisy engine. He turned the Plymouth around with some difficulty and headed back toward Mazatlán. Chris noted the stiff set of his shoulders.

"Is anything the matter, Luis?"

"Matter, señor?"

"You seem, well, uncomfortable."

"I have my worries."

"Yes, well, I guess we all do."

"Where do you want to go, señor?"

"I want someone who deals in silver."

Luis swung around in the seat and looked at him. "Silver?"

"Yes. I think you know what I need it for."

"Mazatlán is not a good place for silver. Taxco is much better."

Chris began to lose patience. "Well, I'm not in Taxco, I'm in Mazatlán. I need a knife made of silver, and I need it now. So take me to a silversmith, or let me get out and I'll find somebody who will."

Luis turned back to the road. His heavy shoulders rose and fell with another sigh. "*Sí,* señor."

They drove on into the city of Mazatlán and along Olas Altas Boulevard, where most of the big hotels and expensive restaurants were built. Luis pulled off on a side street, made another turn, and rolled slowly along a narrow avenue of crowded tourist shops and street vendors. There were art stores with bright bullfight paintings stacked out in front, guitar stores, shops stacked to the roof with wickerware, souvenir stands with red plaster bulls and painted *maracas.* Along the sidewalk, men and women displayed trays of turquoise jewelry and watches, stacks of sombreros and armloads of serapes.

Chris muttered to himself as he searched the store fronts for a likely looking sign.

"You see, señor," said Luis, "in Mazatlán is not so easy to find somebody to make you something of silver."

"I can't believe that," Chris said. "Keep driving."

In the next block he spotted a narrow shop with a neatly lettered sign in the window that read: *JEWELRY MADE TO ORDER.*

"Stop here," he said.

Luis double parked in front of the shop and Chris got out.

"Wait for me," he said.

On the sidewalk in front of the shop two little boys rushed up to Chris offering to sell him gum or plastic flowers. An old woman huddled under blankets shuffled along the pavement carrying a basket of withered fruit. She held out a blackened banana toward Chris. He brushed past the old woman and the boys and entered the jewelry store.

A salesman dressed in a neat dark suit hurried forward to greet him. "Good morning, sir. May I help you?"

"Possibly." Chris glanced down at the display case. It contained pieces of jewelry that looked to be of good quality. "Do you do work in silver?"

"Yes, sir. We have a fine craftsman here who will make up any piece to your order. Is it for a gentleman or a lady?"

"I'm not looking for jewelry," Chris said.

"Oh?"

"What I want is a knife. A knife with a blade of silver."

The man's eyes clouded. The smile gradually faded away. "A knife," he repeated flatly.

"That's right. I don't care what kind of a handle it has, but I want the blade to be silver, and I want it about six inches long."

"That is impossible."

"Why? If your man is as good as you say working with jewelry, surely he can make a knife blade and fit it to a handle."

"I am sorry, he does not do that kind of work."

"Can I talk to him myself?"

"He is not here. He is sick. He will not be in today. Probably not the rest of the week."

Chris looked into the eyes of the jewelry salesman. The man's gaze slid away and darted around the room.

"I'm sure you can buy a knife in any of the souvenir stores along this street."

"Not the kind I want," Chris said.

The salesman moved back behind the display case. "I'm sorry. There is nothing I can do for you."

Chris hesitated for a moment, then turned on his heel and strode out of the store. He marched across the sidewalk to Luis' taxi, and did not see how closely the old woman fruit-vendor watched him. He started to get into the car, but Luis reached out and placed a hand on his arm.

"I am sorry, señor, I can no longer drive you."

"What do you mean?"

"I have other business."

Chris started to protest, but Luis started the engine, and the taxi began to edge away. The stocky driver looked back once with a strange sadness in his eyes. "I am sorry, señor. *Adiós.*"

Luis stepped on the accelerator and the old Plymouth roared up the street. Puzzled, Chris stood looking after the car. Behind him the old lady in the blankets moved with surprising vigor as she entered the jewelry store.

Chris began to walk down the crowded street. He had a feeling that eyes were following him from all sides, but whenever he turned to look no one was watching him. The difference in Luis Zarate today troubled him. He also wondered about the strange actions of the jewelry salesman. A sense of growing urgency prickled the hair at the back of his neck.

He had walked not quite a block when a hand dropped on his shoulder from behind. He spun around and was surprised to see the salesman from the jewelry store. The man pushed a folded piece of paper into Chris's hand.

"Here you will find what you are looking for," he said. "I cannot say more." With a nervous glance at the people passing them on the sidewalk, the man turned and hurried back toward the store.

Chris unfolded the paper and read: *Tulio Santos, 48 Calle Verde*. The man from the store was out of sight when he looked up.

The thought came to him at once that it might be some kind of trap. People were acting much too strangely today. And yet, what else did he have? Time was passing, and tonight was the full moon.

He hailed a passing taxi, this one a red Ford, somewhat newer than Luis Zarate's Plymouth. He showed the handwritten note to the driver.

"Calle Verde? You sure you wan' to go there, man?"

"Why not?"

"It's a bad street for tourists. It's a bad street for anybody."

"I'll take my chances," Chris said, getting in. "Let's go."

26

THE STREET CALLED Calle Verde was still another side of Mazatlán. It bore no resemblance to the moneyed boulevard that curved along the shore, nor the gaudy tourist streets just inland. Calle Verde was a narrow, grubby passage, between rows of weatherstained buildings which gave no evidence of life within. The few people visible on the street moved furtively, as though they expected to be stopped and searched at any moment. A quarter of a mile away was the blighted section called La Ratonera. Some of its human refuse spilled over into Calle Verde.

The cab driver pulled to a stop. "This is it, man, if you still want it."

"Where?" Chris said. "I don't see any numbers."

"There." The driver pointed to a scabrous wooden building with a blind doorway, where a hollow-cheeked little boy sat playing with a piece of string.

Chris got out of the cab and paid the driver. The child watched him, his young eyes already narrow with suspicion. Chris stepped past the silent boy and pushed through the door into a dark, musty room that looked like the overflow from a junkyard. There was a long workbench along one wall. Both the bench and the floor were littered with blackened pots and pans, dented kettles, tarnished, mismatched pieces of silverware, tools, nails, bits of wire, and odd chunks of metal.

"Anybody here?" Chris called.

After a minute a bald, monkey-faced man appeared from somewhere in the rear.

"Tulio Santos?"

"*Sí.*"

"*Habla usted inglés?*"

"No."

Chris switched to his laborious high-school Spanish. "*Quiero comprar un cuchillo. Un cuchillo de plata.*"

The bald-headed man came closer and peered into Chris's face. "A knife of silver," he repeated, speaking Spanish very slowly for the benefit of the gringo.

"Yes."

"For what?"

"That is of no matter. I will pay your price."

Santos pursed his lips; that made him look more than ever like a monkey. "Ah. Well. A knife of silver. A moment." He vanished again into the gloom at the back of the big room. In a little while he came back carrying a tiny, flat butter knife. He displayed it proudly for Chris. "Here. A knife of silver."

"No, no," Chris said impatiently. "A *knife*." He looked around for something to draw on. He found a crumpled sheet of brown wrapping paper and smoothed it out on the work bench. With his ballpoint pen he sketched the outline of a long, vicious knife with an upturned, Bowie-type blade. Then gripping the end of his pen like the hilt of a dagger, he made stabbing motions in the air. "A *knife*," he said again. "Like this. You understand?"

Santos watched him slice the air with his pen, then studied the drawing for a long minute. At last he looked up and shook his head. "I have nothing like this. Not of silver."

"Can you make one?"

Another long study of the drawing, with much frowning and many shakes of the bald head. "Perhaps. But it will be very dear."

"I will pay your price," Chris said. He opened his wallet to show the bills inside. "Make the knife."

Santos looked up from the wallet to Chris's face. He nodded slowly, then turned and walked to a pile of debris in one corner of the room. He began digging through the accumulated junk.

Chris watched the second hand sweep around the

face of his watch, and willed the man to hurry. After five minutes Santos gave a cry of discovery. With his sleeve he rubbed the dirt off his find and held it up to show Chris. It was an ornate, badly tarnished silver tea tray.

"*La plata*," said Santos proudly.

"No, no," said Chris, thinking he still had not made himself understood. "I want a knife." Again he went through the stabbing pantomime. "A knife."

Santos bobbed his head up and down. "Yes, I comprehend. A knife." With a blackened forefinger he outlined on the tray the shape of the blade Chris had drawn."

"You will make a knife from the tray?"

"Yes, yes." Santos grinned happily for a moment, then his smile faded. "It will not be a good knife. The silver is too soft for a blade. It will not cut."

"It is of no matter," said Chris. "Make the knife."

Santos cleared a space on the workbench and set the silver tray on it. He shuffled about the room, gathering up his tools. To Chris's eyes the man moved with agonizing slowness.

The soft knock on the door of Cabana Number 7 surprised Audrey. She had not expected Chris back until later in the afternoon. She had intended to be freshly bathed and perfumed and dressed in her most flattering clothes. She wanted him to be acutely aware of what a beautiful young woman he was treating so shabbily. But here she was still in her robe, and without her hair fully brushed out. Luckily, she had at least recovered from the hangover. Audrey belted the robe, smoothed it over her breasts and hips, and opened the door.

It was not Chris who stood outside. It was instead a tall, lithe woman with intense green eyes and shoulder-length black hair shot with a streak of silver.

"Hello, Audrey," said Marcia Lura.

Audrey stared. She felt held in place by the woman's gaze. "Do I know you?"

"No, but we have acquaintances in common."

"Who?"

"Chris Halloran, for one. For another, the woman now calling herself Karyn Richter."

Audrey curled her lip. "Oh, that one."

"I do not like her any more than you," Marcia said.

"Uh, come in," Audrey said uncertainly. "I was just about to get dressed."

Marcia stepped into the room and eased the door shut behind her. She glanced around without interest, then turned her luminiscent green eyes on Audrey once more. "Would you like to have Karyn Richter out of your life for good? And out of Chris Halloran's life?"

"Well—sure, I guess so."

"I can help you."

"Why? Why would you help me?"

"It is for myself too. I have an old score to settle with that woman."

Audrey felt a strange weakness in her knees. Her mind was sluggish as the woman's smoky voice and unblinking eyes pushed away all outside thoughts.

"What do you want me to do?"

Marcia took the younger woman's hand and drew her down on the wicker settee. As she spoke, Marcia let her hand rest lightly on Audrey's thigh. Audrey was intensely aware of the heat of the hand through the thin material of her robe.

"I have learned that the woman Karyn is out now in the glass-bottomed boat," Marcia said. "When she returns you will give her a message."

"A message," Audrey repeated dully. The strange woman's touch was awakening new, wild sensations in her.

"You will tell her that Chris Halloran returned while she was out, and could not wait for her. You will say that Chris wants her to come at once to the cabin of the gypsy. He will be there waiting for her."

"The cabin of the gypsy? Where's that?"

"She will know," Marcia said. "Tell her it is of life-and-death importance that she go there at once to meet him."

"I don't understand," Audrey said.

Marcia's hand moved along her leg. "When this Karyn arrives at the cabin, there will be a surprise waiting for her. Someone from her past. Someone who will see to it that she breaks up no more happy couples."

The woman's words had little meaning for Audrey. The important thing was the delicious touch of her hand. When Audrey spoke, it was in a throaty whisper. "What if Chris comes back before I can give her the message?"

Marcia turned on the sofa to face her. As though by accident, her hand slipped under the edge of the robe. For a moment it rested there on the smooth, bare flesh of Audrey's inner thigh. Then the hand moved, now with more assurance, sliding up to the moist nest of hair between her legs. Audrey sucked in her breath.

"Chris won't come back early," Marcia said. "I have seen to it that he will be detained."

"All right," Audrey said. Her hips rolled, moving against the light pressure of the woman's hand.

"The boat will return in less than an hour," Marcia said. "You will give Karyn the message as soon as she steps off."

"Yes," Audrey whispered. Her mind swam. Her body was responding to this woman as though with a will of its own. Her own hand moved down and covered Marcia's. Together, their fingers slipped in past the moist vaginal lips.

Breathing rapidly, Audrey said, "Will she believe me?"

Marcia's slender, sensitive fingers found the secret place, and Audrey gasped.

"You can make her believe you," Marcia said. She probed deeply, gently, insistently. "Have you something that belongs to Chris Halloran? Something very private and personal? Something he might send to this Karyn to convince her his message is genuine?"

Audrey tried to think. It was difficult with the waves of sensation that pulsed through her from the other woman's caress. "I—I do have one thing. I can show it to you."

She moved to rise, but found she could not. She looked helplessly into the green eyes.

Marcia smiled at her. "It's all right, dear. We have enough time." Slowly she drew her hand from between Audrey's legs with a soft, sucking sound. With her green eyes never leaving Audrey's face, she raised her fingers to her lips and tasted them.

Feeling unsteady on her feet, Audrey walked carefully across the room to the bureau. She pulled out the top drawer and removed her jewel box. With numb fingers she fumbled through the rings and bracelets, and finally came up with what she wanted—the misshapen silver bullet that had fallen out of Chris's pocket the other day.

Marcia rose from the sofa and walked over to stand beside her. "Did you find it?"

"Yes. I don't know why, but this seemed to have

a special meaning for him." Audrey held out the bullet in her open palm to the other woman.

Marcia recoiled as though it were a tarantula. Audrey looked at her in surprise, but she recovered quickly.

"That will serve very well," Marcia said. "Yes, that will be perfect."

She smiled a dark, secret smile that frightened Audrey for a moment, but then it was gone, and Marcia was again looking at her in that knowing woman's way.

Audrey set the lump of silver down gently on the bureau and turned so she was facing Marcia. She could not speak, but her body cried out its need.

The tip of Marcia's tongue slipped out and ran around her pale lips. She reached out and undid the belt of Audrey's robe. The robe fell open, and Marcia's eyes moved over her body like a caress.

"Yes, dear Audrey," she said, "we have almost an hour to spend together." She slipped an arm around the girl's naked waist and led her to the bed.

27

ON CALLE VERDE, the minutes dragged slowly on into the afternoon. Nervous sweat soaked through Chris Halloran's shirt under both arms and between the shoulder blades. He paced constantly about the big musty room while Tulio Santos worked with saw, hammer, and file to fashion a knife blade from the silver tea tray.

He came to a stop behind Santos and watched the man slowly, slowly shape the cutting edge of the blade. "Can't you speed it up?" he said, then groped for the Spanish words. *"Puede usted trabaja mas rápido?"*

Santos turned and looked at him with an injured expression. "Señor," he said formally, *"estoy un artesano, no mecánico."*

"All right, all right, I'm sorry," Chris said. "Just—continue."

Santos nodded gravely and went back to his work.

At the small dock below the Palacio del Mar Hotel the glass-bottomed boat eased into its mooring. It stopped with a soft bump as the wooden dock nudged the old automobile tires lashed to the side of the boat. Karyn stood up on the deck and searched the faces of the people waiting on shore, looking for Chris Halloran. He was not there. Karyn was surprised, however, to see Audrey Vance. The girl was standing apart from the people waiting to take the next cruise. She looked directly at Karyn.

The gangplank was lowered and Karyn crossed to the dock. Audrey came toward her at once. There was an odd brightness in the girl's eyes, but Audrey did not seem to have been drinking.

"Hi," Audrey said. She smiled tentatively.

Karyn did not return the smile. She nodded in greeting and waited for the girl to say whatever was on her mind.

"Karyn, I don't blame you for thinking I'm a bitch," Audrey said. "God knows I've acted like one. It was plain, childish jealousy. I'm ashamed of myself, really I am. I didn't understand the way it was between you and Chris."

"Don't worry about it," Karyn said.

"I'm awfully glad you feel that way. I wish you

and I could have got off to a better start. I think we might have been friends. I was just telling Chris that."

"Chris is here?"

"No. He came back from town while you were out on the boat, but he had to leave again right away. He asked me to give you a message."

"What message?"

"He said he wants you to come and meet him at the cabin of the gypsy. I don't know what he meant, but he said you would understand."

Karyn stared at the younger woman. Why would Chris trust her with an important message like this? Maybe there was no one else. . . .

"Chris said it was urgent," Audrey went on. "As a matter of fact, he said life and death. He wouldn't tell me any more, but I know he was deadly serious."

"You say he wants me to go to the gypsy's cabin?" Karyn repeated. "Right away?"

"That's what he said. Repeated it several times to make sure I had it right."

Karyn calculated rapidly. It was now early afternoon. If she started immediately she could reach the cabin before dark, but she could never complete the return trip. Chris must have an awfully good reason for subjecting both of them to the danger of night in the mountains.

"He didn't say anything else?" she asked. "Give you a reason?"

Audrey shook her head. "Oh, I almost forgot." She dug into a pocket of her snug white jeans. "Chris said I should give you this. That you would know what it meant."

Karyn took the lump of silver metal from the girl's hand. A bullet. Scarred and misshapen, but unmistakably one of the silver bullets Chris had made to fight the wolves of Drago. What did it mean? That he was successful in getting a new weapon? But what had that to do with the gypsy's cabin? Whatever the meaning, the silver bullet convinced Karyn that the message came from Chris.

"What's it all about, Karyn?" Audrey asked, her eyes wide.

"I'm not sure myself," Karyn said distractedly. She started for the hotel, then turned back. "Thank you, Audrey. Thanks for the message."

"Heck, that's all right. Listen, is there anything I can do to help?"

"No. No, there's nothing. Excuse me now, I have to get going."

Karyn hurried up the slope toward the hotel. She did not see Audrey's small, cold smile as the girl watched her go.

There were no other messages for her at the desk. She went to her room and hurriedly changed to outdoor clothes. She prayed that there would be good news when she met Chris at the cabin. That the long nightmare would be over.

Back out in front of the hotel she looked for the

taxi of Luis Zarate, but the old Plymouth was not there. She would like to have had Luis, but there was no time to try to find him. Another cab drove up. A middle-aged couple got out, wearing straw sombreros with *MAZATLAN* lettered across the brims. Karyn hurried up to the driver.

"Do you know a man called Guillermo, the one who keeps the burros for riding in the mountains?"

"I know him."

"Will you take me there?"

"The road to Guillermo's place is very bad. I will have to charge extra."

"I don't care. Just take me there."

Karyn did not wait for the driver to open the door for her. She got in and slammed it firmly behind her. The man backed the taxi around and started off toward the highway.

At last the knife was finished. Chris had been eager to take the weapon the moment Santos finished shaping the cutting edge of the blade. It was seven inches of businesslike metal with a thin, bare, four-inch shank for the handle. However, Santos had heatedly refused to turn it over without a proper handle. Angry at first, Chris had cooled down when he saw the practicality of this. For the purpose he intended the knife, a solid grip would be essential.

So he had sweated out another half-hour while Santos dug up a rusted hunting knife from somewhere among the refuse. The craftsman dismantled the old knife, took the carved wooden handle with finger grips and affixed it solidly to the silver blade.

Santos was still not satisfied with the balance of the weapon, but Chris took it away from him and peeled off several bills in payment. Santos gave him the leather sheath with belt loop that had gone with the hunting knife. Chris slipped the silver blade into the sheath, fastened it in, and hurried out into the street.

He had expected to hail a taxi immediately to take him back to the hotel, but the street was deserted. Not only was there no taxi in sight, there were no moving vehicles of any kind. Chris wheeled and ran back into the shop of Tulio Santos.

"Necesitamo un taxi!"

Santos shook his head and smiled sadly. *"No taxi aquí. Nunca taxi en Calle Verde."*

Chris swore under his breath. *"Hay teléfono?"* Again Santos shook his head.

"Damn," Chris muttered. He went back out to the street. The building fronts were blank, the doors closed, the windows shuttered and forbidding. Shadows were growing longer as night moved in on the city.

Chris slammed a fist into his open palm. By this time Karyn would be wondering what was keeping him. One thing was certain—standing here on this empty, darkening street would gain him nothing.

He started to run. He headed west, because that's

where the city was. There were bound to be taxis, policemen, something. The silver knife in its sheath bounced against his hip. As he ran he made sure he did not lose the weapon. He knew that somewhere tonight he was going to have to use it.

28

THE TAXI CARRYING Karyn Richter jolted up the rutted road that led into the hills. The driver complained steadily of the damage the trip was inflicting on his automobile. After a drive that seemed like hours to Karyn, they pulled up at the dry arroyo where the road ended and Guillermo had his shack.

"This is where you wanted to go, lady," said the driver.

"Yes, thank you." Karyn started to get out of the car.

"That's ten dollars."

Karyn gave him a look, but there was no time to argue about the fare. She dug a bill out of her pocket and handed it to the man. She left the car and hurried across the expanse of gravel and bare dirt to the door of the shack. She rapped loudly on the patchwork-lumber door, but heard no response from inside.

"Hello!" she called. "Guillermo! Anybody here?"

Still no sounds from inside the shack. Karyn pushed on the door, but it would not budge. She walked around to the back. Half a dozen burros stood placidly in a rude pen. They looked at her without curiosity. Guillermo was nowhere in sight.

From out in front of the shack came the sudden sound of an engine revving up, followed by the spinning of tires in loose gravel. Karyn ran back around the corner of the building in time to see her taxi bouncing away down the road toward the city.

"Thanks a lot," she muttered after the disppearing cab.

She drew a deep breath and told herself to be calm and consider her circumstances. A ride back to the city was now out of the question. In the late afternoon, it was doubtful whether she could make it back to the highway and civilization before nightfall. When night came she did not want to be alone.

Riding a burro, she could reach the gypsy's cabin before dark, barring mishap. Chris would be at the cabin, according to his message, so that seeme dthe safest way to go.

She walked back around to the rear of the shack where the burros were kept. She found a pile of old blankets, folded one, and placed it over the back of a burro. She opened the gate to the pen, led the animal out, and closed the gate behind her. She climbed on the burro, urged it forward, and with some reluctance the animal started up the trail.

As she rode, the shadow that preceded her up the mountain grew ever longer. It was a constant reminder of the coming night, and of all the horrors that the night could bring.

Karyn pulled her mind away from those thoughts. She thought instead about Chris and herself and what their futures would be. It would not be a future together—they had tried that once and it had been disastrous. Besides, she had a husband and a little boy to go back to when this business was finished. And what about Chris? Would he go back to Audrey? Or a series of Audreys? Somehow Karyn did not think so. She had seen, these past few days, a maturity in Chris which had been lacking in him before. She hoped with all her heart that he would find happiness.

With agonizing slowness the little burro plodded up the trail. They passed the spring where she and Chris had stopped to rest the last time. No time for resting now. She clucked in the burro's ear and urged it onward.

The shadows closed in fast, and the sun was red and angry on the western horizon when they finally reached the crest where the gypsy Philina had her cabin. The rude log building looked like blessed sanctuary to Karyn. There was no sign of life, but as before, smoke trailed out of the hole in the roof.

Why, she wondered, was Chris not outside to greet her? Maybe he was inside talking to Philina and hadn't heard the burro come up.

Karyn dismounted and walked toward the door of the cabin. Her steps slowed as she sensed something different here. The doorway was uncovered, that was it. The animal hide that had hung there before was gone. Cautiously, she approached and peered into the cabin. A flickering red-orange light from the firepit danced over the interior walls. She stopped just outside the doorway.

"Chris? Is anybody there?"

All at once she knew it was wrong. It was all wrong. The cabin did not look right. The burro-keeper should have been down below; the message from Chris rang false. Everything was wrong, and she'd realized it too late. She started to back away. One step. Then another.

Before Karyn could take a third step, a slim, strong arm encircled her throat, clamping her windpipe in the crook of the elbow. She fought to scream, but no sound could escape. She clawed at the arm that was cutting off her breath, but she could not move it.

The world began to go dark. Karyn felt the strength ebbing from her like blood from a severed vein. Red flashes of fireworks burst somewhere behind her eyes. A roaring like the wind filled her ears.

Then blackness.

29

FOR CHRIS HALLORAN, the run through the dreary back streets of Mazatlán began to take on the quality of a nightmare. It was as though all other living things had been snatched from the face of the earth. The only sound was the thud and scuff of his feet on the pavement.

After many blocks he spotted a taxi parked at the curb. The cab was empty, but from a nearby doorway came the sound of recorded music. Chris pushed aside a curtain hanging over the doorway and walked in.

It was a dim, musty *cantina*, stale with cigarette smoke and old chiles. A thirty-year-old jukebox played a tragic Mexican ballad. Along the bar sat several men in faded, mismatched clothing. Their eyes slid over Chris without expression. At a table in the rear, two women, heavily made up for the approaching evening, sat nursing glasses of tequila. They turned their professional smiles on him, but their eyes were empty of hope.

Chris paid no attention to the customers. He leaned on the unvarnished bar and spoke to the man in shirtsleeves who stood behind it.

"Hay cochero aquí?"

The proprietor did not speak, but looked down the bar. One of the customers, a thin man with moles on his cheek, spoke up. "I am the owner of the taxi."

"Will you take me to the Palacio del Mar?"

The man turned lazily back to the bar. "Sure. When I finish my drink."

Chris took a step toward him. His eyes glittered dangerously. "Take me *now*."

The unmistakable menace in Chris's voice got through. *"Sí,* señor," the driver said automatically. In a gulp he downed what was left in his glass and walked quickly with Chris out to the cab. He drove well and swiftly, and they pulled up in front of the hotel fifteen minutes later.

The crowd at the Palacio del Mar had increased since that morning. Sightseers wandered about snapping pictures and talking in excited voices about *"la cabana de la muerte."*

Chris paid off the driver and hurried up the steps, across the veranda, and into the lobby. Señor

Davila, the manager, was at his post behind the desk. He was relating, with dramatic emphasis, the events of the bloody night to a small, attentive group of tourists.

Chris pushed to the front of the group and got Davila's attention. "Ring Mrs. Richter's room," he said.

Reluctantly the manager turned away from his audience long enough to operate the key that would ring the telephone in Karyn's room. He rang several times, then turned to Chris with an apologetic shrug.

"Señora Richter does not answer."

"She must be there," Chris insisted. "What time did the cruise boat get back?"

"About noon."

"Have you seen Mrs. Richter since then?"

"I—I don't remember."

"Well, *think* about it." Chris leaned on the desk and glared at Davila.

The manager chewed his lip nervously. "Ah, yes, I recall now. She did stop by the desk to ask if there were any messages. I told her there were none, and she went up to her room."

"Did she go out again after that?"

"I could not say. Please understand, señor, this has been a very busy day. I could not see everyone that comes and goes."

"Yeah, sure," said Chris. He spun away from the desk and stalked back through the lobby.

Where the devil could she be, he wondered. He walked quickly through the busy bar and the dining room, scanning the faces. Karyn was in neither place.

It did not seem likely she would be on the beach. It was too late in the afternoon for sunbathing. Still, it was a possibility. Chris ran out of the building and down across the crescent of sand to the water's edge. He jogged along the tideline, checking the few people who were in the water and on the beach. No Karyn.

Chris did not like it. Karyn knew he would come looking for her. If she was not going to be easy to find, she would have left a message for him at the desk. Something was definitely wrong.

He stood at the edge of the beach and tried to think of possibilities. Maybe Audrey knew something. Chris loped back across the beach to his cabana. The blinds were down, the door was locked. Chris banged his fist against the panel until Audrey opened up. Her eyes were not quite in focus, and she swayed slightly as she opened the door. Chris could smell liquor on her breath.

"Nice of you to drop by," she said with heavy sarcasm.

Chris pushed past her into the room. The air was stale in the gloom. He walked to the window and snapped up the blind, letting in the afternoon sun.

"Have you seen Karyn?" he said.

"Your lady love? Fuck, no. Why would I see her?"

"I don't have time for bullshit, Audrey. Just give me straight answers."

"You don't have time for much of anything these days, do you, lover boy?"

Audrey knew something. Chris could see it in her eyes. "I'm asking you again, have you seen Karyn? Do you know where she is?"

"Find her yourself, lover boy. A bitch in heat like that one, it shouldn't be hard for you to—"

Chris hit her. A hard, open-handed blow across the side of the face. Audrey staggered backward several steps. She put a hand to her reddening cheek. Tears squeezed out of her eyes.

"Now let's talk," Chris said.

Audrey hiccuped and shook her head. Chris moved toward her, and she began to talk.

"I saw her. She—she's gone."

"Gone? Gone where?"

"I don't know. I just gave her a message, then she went out."

"What message?" Chris said. It was an effort to keep from screaming at her.

"There was a woman here. She said to tell Karyn you wanted her to come and meet you. That's all."

"Who was the woman?"

Audrey's eyes fell away from his, and her voice softened. "I don't know her name. Very pretty. Tall, green eyes, black hair with a streak of white."

Chris ground his teeth. With unerring instinct, Marcia Lura had found the weak point in their defenses. Audrey. Speaking very softly, he said, "Where was Karyn supposed to meet me?"

"I don't remember."

"Audrey, you'll remember or I'll kick the shit out of you."

"It was something about a gypsy. The gypsy's cabin."

Chris swore under his breath. If Karyn had been lured up into those mountains, there was no way she could get back before dark. She would be easy prey for the werewolves, and out of reach of help.

"Didn't she question you when you told her that?" he demanded.

"I—I gave her something of yours so she'd believe the message came from you."

"What did you give her?"

"That little lump of silver you always carried around. The one that looked like a bullet."

Chris's hand went to his pocket. Things had happened so fast the last few days, he hadn't even noticed the bullet was missing. He whirled and started toward the door. He yanked it open, then turned back.

"I'm going out now, Audrey. I don't know how long I'll be gone, but when I come back I don't want to see you here." He went out and slammed the door without waiting for a reply.

The taxi he had come in was gone, but there

was another just turning around in front of the hotel and heading back toward Mazatlán. Chris ran toward the car.

"Taxi! Hey, taxi!"

The driver, with a full load of passengers, ignored him. Chris stood in the roadway cursing after the departing cab.

"Señor?"

The voice close behind him made Chris start. He turned to see Luis Zarate nervously fingering the zipper of his jacket.

"Luis!"

"I came looking for you, señor. I should not have left you today in the city. I am very ashamed."

"Never mind that," Chris said, "I need you now. They've tricked Karyn into going to the gypsy's cabin. I've got to go after her."

A stricken look came over Luis.

"What's the matter?"

"The gypsy, señor. Philina. *Ella está muerte.*"

"She's dead?"

"*Sí*, señor." With a shake of his head, Luis returned to English. "The word was spread today among the gypsies and the people of the streets. Philina is dead, and anyone who helps the gringos will follow her. They will know the vengeance of *lobombre.*"

"That's why the salesman in the jewelry store acted so funny this morning."

Luis nodded.

"And that's why you left me there on the street."

"Yes, but now I am ashamed. My poor taxi is at your service."

"Then let's go. Take me to your cousin's place, the one with the burros."

"Mucho gusto, señor, mucho gusto!"

They roared out of the hotel compound in the old Plymouth and up the highway toward Mazatlán. Luis swerved expertly onto the narrow rutted road leading into the foothills. The car bounced and rattled and seemed at times about to fly to pieces, but Luis never let up on the accelerator. When they raeched the shack of Guillermo the burro keeper Chris jumped out and hit the ground running. Luis followed close behind him.

Chris hammered on the door, but received no response from within.

"Where could he be?" Chris demanded.

Luis stepped forward. "Permit me, señor." He put his mouth close to the door, and in a voice of thunder shouted, *"Guillermo! Nombre de Dios, abre la porta!"*

After a moment there was the sound of something heavy scraping across the floor inside. The door opened a crack, and Guillermo's one good eye peered out.

"What do you want?"

"Has the woman been here?" Chris said. "The woman who came with me last time?"

"She was here."

"When?" Chris's question snapped like a whip.

"Two, three hours ago."

"What did she say to you?"

"She said nothing. I did not open the door."

"Why, for God's sake? What's the matter with you?"

The eye squinted out at Chris from the crack in the door. "There is evil and death in the mountains. It is a time for a poor man like me to stay behind doors."

"Well, where did she go?"

"She took one of my burros and started up the trail."

"Give me a burro," Chris said. "Quickly. I have to go after her."

"I do not think you can help her now."

"I don't give a damn what you think. What about that burro?"

"Go to the back and take one yourself, señor. It will be ten dollars for yours and the lady's."

Chris started to say something, changed his mind. He pulled a bill from his wallet, tossed it at the crack in the door, and started around the shack.

In the pen he found a sturdy-looking burro and led him around to the front. Luis Zarate was standing there by the Plymouth.

"I would go with you, señor," said Luis, "but I have both a wife and a mother who depend on me. And the truth is that I am not a very brave man."

"That's all right, Luis. From here on it's my fight. What do I owe you for the ride?"

"No charge, señor."

"Thanks." Chris climbed on the burro's back and urged the animal up the trail.

"Buena suerte, señor," Luis called after him. *"Vaya con Dios."*

He would need more than luck this time, Chris thought as the burro jogged toward the mountains. Maybe even the company of God would not be enough. He rode upward into the gathering darkness.

30

THE PAIN CAME BACK first. Pain in her throat. In the instant before she regained consciousness, Karyn was a little girl again. She was lying on a high, white bed in the hospital, and the doctor had just taken her tonsils out. In a moment she would open her eyes and her mother would be there. And Daddy. And they would let her eat all the ice cream she wanted, and before long the pain would go away.

Karyn tried to reach up with a hand and touch her throat where it hurt. But the hand would not move. Her lungs heaved, pulling in air, but it did not have the sharp, clean smell of the hospital. The roughness against her back was no bed.

She forced her eyes open. No loving faces looked

down on her. It took only a moment for her to realize where she was. In the gypsy's cabin. The light from the fire pit cast grotesque shadows throughout the room. Karyn was sitting in the chair with no back. Her ankles were tied to the legs of the chair, her wrists tightly bound behind her. The roughness against her back was the log wall of the cabin.

She turned her head. It hurt her throat when she moved. Beside her was the pile of old rags where Philina the gypsy had sat talking to her and Chris such a little while ago. Beyond the rags she could see another torn bundle. Only the clawed hand, lying limp and palm up, told her that it had once been human.

Karyn looked away quickly. Through the open doorway the world outside was in deepening twilight. Someone stepped between her and the doorway. A tall, slim silhouette with flowing black hair that was shot through with silver.

"Marcia!" Karyn's voice was a rasping whisper.

"I see you remember me. I'm glad. You will have much time for remembering in the hours before dawn."

"What do you mean?"

"I'm going to hurt you, Karyn. I'm going to hurt you very badly."

Karyn squinted in the darkness, trying to get a better look at the woman. "Why? Why are you doing this? Why are you persecuting me? You took my husband from me back in Drago. What more do you want?" She broke off as the effort of talking hurt her throat too much.

Marcia took a step toward her. The fire pit lay between them. The tall woman knelt so the light of the fire shone full on her face. "You want to know why, do you? Then look!"

She raised a hand to her forehead and ran long fingers through the white streak in her midnight hair. "This is why. I have this mark to remind me of the night you put the gun inches from my head and fired. I will never forget the agony of that moment and the long months that followed. In those months, Karyn, I thought of you above all else. I have lived for just one thing—to give you some measure of the pain I felt. And finally to see you die."

"I had to shoot that night," Karyn whispered. "I saw only a wolf. I couldn't know it was you."

"You lie!" the other woman spat. "Just before you pulled the trigger I heard you speak my name. Oh, yes, you knew."

It was true, Karyn realized. In that long-ago night when she fired the silver bullet into the head of the sleek black wolf, she had known full well it was the woman Marcia Lura. What a tragic shame that the creature had not died.

"I have had much time to think," Marcia went on. "In that time I have imagined many ways for you to die. In all of them you suffered greatly. And now things have worked out even better than I could imagine. Now I can kill you in a most appropriate way."

Marcia reached down to the edge of the fire pit. There the taped ends of a long-handled pair of pliers protruded from the fire. The other end, with the pincer jaws, was buried deep in the glowing coals.

"In the Middle Ages," Marcia said, "there were many interesting ways of dealing with people suspected of being witches. Or werewolves." She lightly caressed the taped handles of the pliers as she spoke. "One of the ways was to use a red-hot pair of tongs to pull the flesh from the body of the victim. A pinch at a time. It takes a very long time for someone to die that way. Very long, and very painful." She looked up and the fire struck glowing red sparks in the deep green eyes. "That, Karyn, is the way you are going to die tonight."

Karyn pulled her eyes away from the woman, and from the vicious tool jammed deep into the coals. She looked toward the open doorway. Outside the twilight had deepened to the charcoal gray of approaching night.

Marcia saw the direction of her glance. "If you're expecting help from your friend Chris or anyone else tonight, you're going to be disappointed. Even if he does learn where you are and foolishly comes after you, he will never reach us. There is only one trail to this cabin, and someone is waiting for your friend on that trail. Someone you and I both know very well."

"Roy!" The name tore at Karyn's throat as she spoke it.

The other woman smiled. A slow smile of triumph. "Yes, Roy. Your husband once, but not any more. Now he is mine. He belongs to me more completely than ever he did to you. He will be there to meet anyone who comes up the trail, and he will see that you and I are left alone."

Karyn stared at the dark woman. Fear rose like bile in her aching throat. Slowly, slowly Marcia drew the long pliers from the fire. The cruel pinchers glowed a bright red-orange.

Without warning, one side of Marcia's face jerked for an instant in a tic brought on by violent emotion. She threw one quick look over her shoulder, then came around the fire pit toward Karyn. She gripped the handles of the pliers and thrust the glowing-hot jaws before her.

31

THE LAST RED SLICE of the sun slipped below
the horizon, and night came all at once on the trail
leading up the mountain. Chris swore at his failure
to bring a flashlight. He could still make out the
trail itself, but the deep shadows at either side could
have concealed anything. To the little burro, day
or night made no difference. He plodded patiently
upward, breaking into a jog occasionally as Chris
dug in his heels.

He tried not to think about what he might find
when he reached the gypsy's cabin. The old woman
was dead, that much Luis had told him. He did not
say the werewolves had killed her, but the implica-
tion was clear. What would Karyn have found at
the cabin? Would she panic? He could only hope

273

that Karyn had locked herself inside when darkness came, and would stay there until he arrived.

With no details visible in the darkness, it was difficult for Christ to calculate how far he had come. Since the afternoon, he had paid no attention to time and distance, except for the position of the sun. He had been on the trail almost two hours before darkness fell. By now, he reckoned, he should be nearing the crest where the cabin was. He prayed he would find Karyn there alive and unhurt. Together they had a chance to survive this night. Separately—

The thought died in Chris's mind. Subtly, a change came over the mountain trail and the brush alongside. Details became visible as the blackness gave way gradually to a cool, pale light. He looked up through a gap in the trees and saw the round, bland face of the moon edging into view above the ridge of mountains.

With more light, the climb became easier, but the coming of the moon reminded Chris of the horror he must yet face this night.

The burro stopped as though someone had jerked him back on a rope. His ears swiveled to catch a sound, his nostrils widened, testing the air. Chris urged him on, but with a frightened bray the burro moved stiffly backward.

"Up, burro, come on," Chris coaxed. "Don't go spooky on me now."

The burro refused to move forward even when

Chris slapped his rump. The animal shivered and showed the whites of its eyes.

"What's the matter, burro? What is it?"

Something moved on the trail up ahead. A shadow eased toward them into the moonlight that now illuminated the trail. The shadow stopped and waited. A huge tan wolf.

The burro bucked and shied away. Its hoofs slipped on lose dirt and the animal fell heavily to the ground. Chris pushed himself away in time to avoid falling under the burro. He heard it scramble upright and go thudding back down the mountain. He was alone on the trail with the wolf.

For a long moment the man and the animal looked at each other. As the wolf moved, the muscles rippled under its shaggy tan pelt. It growled softly, and the teeth gleamed in the moonlight.

Chris reached for the knife, but he was too slow. Before his hand closed over the hilt, the wolf crouched and sprang. Shocked by the suddenness of the attack, Chris dived forward and skidded in the dirt on his chest. He felt the night air stir as the long, powerful body of the wolf passed over him. He scrambled into a crouch as the wolf hit the ground and whirled to come at him again.

Chris slipped the knife out of the leather sheath. He held it out between them so the silver blade glinted under the moon. The pale eyes of the wolf followed the arc of the knife as Chris swung it slowly from side to side. The wolf growled again, deeply and menacingly.

"You know what this is, don't you?" Chris said. "You know what it can do. Now, come and get me if you can."

The wolf lunged forward, Chris thrust at the animal with the knife. The wolf stopped inches away from the blade. Chris slashed out, and the wolf backed off just out of reach.

Again the wolf sprang at him without warning. Chris fell to his right just in time to avoid the slashing teeth, but he was unable to bring the knife around. The wolf landed, spun, and leaped at him again without pausing.

As Chris dived frantically out of the path of the hurtling body something tore away the sleeve of his jacket. In a moment of panic Chris felt his shoulder. There was no blood. He knew too well what the bite of a werewolf could do.

Once more the wolf hesitated, watching, waiting for an opening. He circled Chris in stiff, sideways steps, eyes never leaving the silver blade. Chris turned slowly, keeping the knife always between them, the blade pointed at the throat of the wolf.

For timeless minutes the battle continued, with first man, then beast, feinting, lunging, striking. The wolf was wary of a straight-on attack, and time after time Chris slipped away by inches from the murderous teeth. However, he could not get into position to strike a telling blow with the knife.

As the fight wore on, the superior strength and stamina of the wolf began to tell. Chris's breath came in ragged gasps. His body was bruised from hitting the stones on the trail. Every time the wolf attacked he came a fraction closer. Chris could feel the heat of its breath as the teeth slashed at his face.

He would have to finish it soon, Chris knew, while he still had strength to drive the knife home. He could no longer afford to let the wolf set the pace of the battle.

As he and the wolf faced each other, motionless for the moment, he decided upon a plan. He would feint to one side to draw a reaction from the wolf, then leap on the animal's back and pray he could sink the knife into a vital spot. If he failed—well, one way or another, it would all be over in seconds.

Chris began his sideways feint, but that was as far as he got with his plan. His foot came down on a loose rock the size of a tennis ball, and the ankle bent sharply outward. A dull pain gripped the lower part of his leg. He fought for his balance, lost it, and crashed to the ground. His right hand was flung out to the side, and the back of it struck a sharp-edged rock. The fingers loosened their grip for a moment, and the precious knife fell away.

Before Chris could move to retrieve the weapon, the wolf was upon him. The heavy forepaws pinned his shoulders to the ground. The bristling tan muzzle and killer teeth were just above his face. In the eyes of the wolf there was a gleam of triumph—and something else.

Unable to move, Chris waited for the last searing pain and stared up into the eyes of the beast. Deep in the yellow irises was the shadow of some emotion that did not belong. Sadness?

Unaccountably, the wolf hesitated. Instead of tearing out the man's unprotected throat, it stayed poised over him. Then, ever so gradually, Chris felt the weight on his shoulders ease. He was able to move his right hand. His fingers searched around in the dirt. They closed over the carved handle of the knife.

The pressure returned as the wolf brought his weight down once more on the man's shoulders. The jaws gaped, the teeth moved for the man's throat.

Willing every remaining ounce of strength into the muscles of his right arm and shoulder, Chris drove the knife upward. The silver blade buried itself in the broad chest above him. The wolf's great head jerked back, and from the throat came a howl of dreadful pain that was neither animal nor human. The hot blood of the wolf spilled down over Chris's hand and wrist, and splashed his jacket. Chris pulled the knife free, but there was no need to strike again. The animal lurched sideways for several steps, then fell.

With an effort Chris pulled himself into a sitting position. The stricken wolf raised its head and looked at him. Then, inch by agonizing inch, the animal dragged itself toward him. Chris gripped the bloody knife, but then he saw there was no more fight in the eyes of the wolf, and he relaxed.

Leaving a smeared trail of blood, the wolf pulled its dying body to the side of the man. The big head rose, and their eyes met. Then the light faded from the yellow eyes, the wolf's head sank down on Chris's knee, and it was over.

Chris laid a hand on the short, thick fur that covered the broad head of the wolf. "Goodbye, old friend," he said softly. "You could have won." There was only the night wind to hear his words.

Painfully Chris rose and tested the ankle. It hurt, but he could walk. He pulled off the blood-spattered jacket and wiped the blade of the knife on the remaining sleeve. Then he spread the jacket over the body of the wolf and limped on toward the gypsy's cabin.

32

THE GLOWING JAWS of the pliers reached out for Karyn like the pincers of some hellish insect. Marcia advanced slowly, her eyes on Karyn's face. Behind her the black rectangle of the doorway lightened gradually. Marcia's step faltered. She turned and looked back. The pale edge of the full moon inched out from behind the ridge of mountains. When Marcia turned back, there was terror mixed with the hatred in her face.

With the heat of the glowing metal on her cheek, Karyn pulled her head away as far as she could. Her body tensed, waiting for the searing pain, but it did not come. Instead, it was Marcia who cried out. Karyn looked at the other woman in surprise, and saw her body jerk and twist as though it were controlled by unseen wires. The pliers flew from Marcia's hand, and she doubled over in agony.

As Karyn watched in horrified fascination, Marcia stumbled and fell to the floor of the cabin. She rolled about in the dirt, tearing at her clothes. The garments ripped away under her slashing fingers, and for a moment the lithe, white body was exposed in the moonlight that now flooded through the doorway. Then she began to change. The white skin twitched and crawled and grew coarse black hair in uneven patches. Her limbs writhed into misshapen things that belonged on neither animal nor human. She continued to roll helplessly on the ground. From the tortured throat came a high-pitched whine.

In the light of the fire Karyn saw the face. There was little left of what had been the beautiful Marcia Lura. The nose had shriveled to a blackened shapeless thing with fat, leaking nostrils. The long black hair, still with the deadly streak of silver, was now a scrubby growth on most of the face. The mouth became a crooked slash, half of it the lipless maw of a wolf, the other half grotesquely human. Only the eyes, the eyes of deep green fire, were unaltered.

The smell of smoke pulled Karyn's attention away from the creature writhing on the floor. Beside her, where the red-hot pliers had fallen, the pile of rags smoldered and caught fire. Flames licked up over the pile hungrily, fed by old oils soaked into the rags, and began to race up the dry log walls.

Karyn made a lunge toward the doorway, but only fell heavily to the dirt floor, still bound to the broken chair. Only a few feet away the thing that had been Marcia jerked and screamed on the ground, driven frantic by the flames.

Karyn strained every muscle, but could make no headway toward the door and safety. With the fire quickly eating away at the cabin, she made a decision, then shut off her mind to the pain that would come. She stretched out her bound wrists behind her as far as she could toward the burning pile of rags. Twisting her head around to look, she saw the skin of her arms redden and blister from the heat. With her teeth biting hard against each other, she forced her hands closer to the flames. A spark danced on the threads of the hemp rope, then another. A puff of flame. Karyn strained, forcing her wrists apart, and with a pop the rope burned through.

Karyn snatched her hands away from the flames and worked with singed fingers at the knots that held her ankles. The fire crackled up three of the four walls now, and fiery streamers raced across the ceiling. The thick, acrid smoke tore at her throat.

At last she solved the knots and was free. Unable to see in the smoke, she stumbled in the direction of the doorway and fell through it to the grass outside with a grateful sob.

Drinking in the clean night air, Karyn dragged herself away from the cabin, now blazing like a torch. From inside the awful screaming sounds rose to a crescendo, then stopped as one of the walls fell in with an explosion of sparks.

From somewhere not far down the mountain came a terrible howl of pain, as though in answer to the death cry of Marcia Lura. Then, except for the crackling flames that consumed the cabin, there was silence.

Someone called Karyn's name.

In sudden fear she turned toward the trail that led up the mountain from below.

"Karyn! Is that you?"

The limping figure of a man came toward her. In the combined light of the moon and the fire she saw that it was Chris Halloran.

"Yes," she said in a hoarse whisper.

"Are you all right?"

"I'm all right." She turned back toward the cabin, where the roof was now gone and the flames were beginning to subside. "Marcia's in there. She's finished now."

"Thank God," said Chris. He dropped wearily to the grass beside her and saw her hands. "You're hurt."

"It will be all right." She searched his face. "On the trail tonight—did you—did you—"

Chris nodded. "Roy was there. He's dead now."

"Then they're both finished. It's over."

Chris turned and looked for a moment back toward the mountain trail. "It's over," he said.

They sat together and watched as the cabin crumbled and the fire burned itself out. Nothing moved in the charred ruin. The night was clear and cold. And silent.

Slowly, Karyn let herself relax. In the days to come there would be much to do, but all she wanted right now was sleep. Sleep with the blessed knowledge that never more would she hear the howling.

Victoria Holt

Here are the stories you love best. Tales about love, intrigue, wealth, power and of course romance. Books that will keep you turning the pages deep into the night.

☐ BRIDE OF PENDORRIC	23280-8	$1.95
☐ THE CURSE OF THE KINGS	23284-0	$1.95
☐ THE HOUSE OF A THOUSAND LANTERNS	23685-4	$1.95
☐ THE KING OF THE CASTLE	23587-4	$1.95
☐ KIRKLAND REVELS	23920-9	$1.95
☐ LEGEND OF THE SEVENTH VIRGIN	23281-6	$1.95
☐ LORD OF THE FAR ISLAND	22874-6	$1.95
☐ MENFREYA IN THE MORNING	23757-5	$1.95
☐ MISTRESS OF MELLYN	23924-1	$1.95
☐ ON THE NIGHT OF THE SEVENTH MOON	23568-0	$1.95
☐ THE PRIDE OF THE PEACOCK	23198-4	$1.95
☐ THE QUEEN'S CONFESSION	23213-1	$1.95
☐ THE SECRET WOMAN	23283-2	$1.95
☐ SHADOW OF THE LYNX	23278-6	$1.95
☐ THE SHIVERING SANDS	23282-4	$1.95

Buy them at your local bookstores or use this handy coupon for ordering:

FAWCETT BOOKS GROUP
P.O. Box C730, 524 Myrtle Ave., Pratt Station, Brooklyn, N.Y. 11205

Please send me the books I have checked above. Orders for less than 5 books must include 75¢ for the first book and 25¢ for each additional book to cover mailing and handling. I enclose $_____ in check or money order.

Name_____

Address_____

City_____ State/Zip_____

Please allow 4 to 5 weeks for delivery.

John D. MacDonald Travis McGee Series

Follow the quests of Travis McGee, amiable and incurable tilter at conformity, boat-bum Quixote, hopeless sucker for starving kittens, women in distress, and large, loose sums of money.

"McGee is top-notch MacDonald."
—Chicago Tribune

FREE
Fawcett Books Listing

There is Romance, Mystery, Suspense, and Adventure waiting for you inside the Fawcett Books Order Form. And it's yours to browse through and use to get all the books you've been wanting... but possibly couldn't find in your bookstore.

This easy-to-use order form is divided into categories and contains over 1500 titles by your favorite authors.

So don't delay—take advantage of this special opportunity to increase your reading pleasure.

Just send us your name and address and 25¢ (to help defray postage and handling costs).

FAWCETT BOOKS GROUP
P.O. Box C730, 524 Myrtle Ave., Pratt Station, Brooklyn, N.Y. 11205

Name_____
(please print)

Address_____
City_____State_____Zip_____
Do you know someone who enjoys books? Just give us their names and addresses and we'll send them an order form too!

Name_____
Address_____
City_____State_____Zip_____

Name_____
Address_____
City_____State_____Zip_____